Grace and Mary

Grace and Mary
MELVYN BRAGG

SCEPTRE

First published in Great Britain in 2013 by Sceptre
An imprint of Hodder & Stoughton
An Hachette UK company

3

A CIP catalogue record for this title is available from the British Library

Hardback ISBN 9781444762341
Trade Paperback ISBN 9781444762358

Typeset by Hewer Text UK Ltd, Edinburgh
Printed and bound by CPI Group (UK) Ltd, Croydon CR0 4YY

Hodder & Stoughton policy is to use papers that are natural, renewable
and recyclable products and made from wood grown in sustainable forests.
The logging and manufacturing processes are expected to conform to the
environmental regulations of the country of origin.

Hodder & Stoughton Ltd
338 Euston Road
London NW1 3BH

www.sceptrebooks.com

To the women who inspired this book.

The mother and son meet mostly in the middle of the last century. After the war. Her disintegrating memory can still take her there and he had been old enough to store up sharp impressions of the life around him. It gives them an illusion of equality. Together they can make that place a time to live in.

It was then that they were mother and child. Now, she is in her tenth decade, he just gone seventy, and slowly the roles are reversing.

More than sixty years have passed, but as her life enters into darkness and silence, they can still draw warmth from the embers of those days. Occasionally they chance the present. Sometimes they sing.

CHAPTER ONE

Mary's voice, thinner now, is still certain and pure, the melody steadily held as she sits up in her bed and sways to the tune, the words coming from the heart as she smiles at him.

> 'Daisy, Daisy, give me your answer do.
> I'm half crazy, all for the love of you.'

He joins in:

> 'It won't be a stylish marriage
> I can't afford a carriage,
> But you'll look sweet,
> Upon the seat,
> Of a bicycle made for two.'

Her laughter, delighted, crystalline, stops abruptly. 'I hope nobody heard us.'

'What if they did?'

'They would throw us out. Throw us right out!'

'They might like it. They might take a collection.'

'The worst thing your father ever did was to get that tandem!'

'Why was that?' Again. He wants the story again. He wants all her stories again.

'Tandems pull ahead of the others! I always wanted to be among them. And when he was on an evening shift, I couldn't go out!' She shrugs, mild now. 'I liked biking a lot more than your dad did.'

'Another mouthful?'

She pulls back her head and looks down on the spoon of ruby-coloured jelly.

'Just one more. Come on!' He pulls his chair a nudge closer to the bed and carefully aims the spoon at her tight lips. The rest of the meal is scarcely touched. 'The last one.' He lets the silence stretch and holds her look.

'Promise?'

'Yes,' he says.

Still she hesitates, eyes him even more intensely, and then swoops, like a bird pecking, jutting out her tongue and, as he tilts the spoon, allows the glistening ruby jelly to slide into her mouth. She swallows it slowly. 'No more!' she cries, covering her mouth with her hand. 'No more!'

He keeps his word.

She looks out of the window a while. 'Look at that beautiful tree,' she says, and adds, in sudden alarm, 'What would we do without trees?' Tears fill her eyes as she appeals to him.

'There'll always be trees.'

'Will there? Oh – will there? Oh, I hope so . . .'

He nods, suddenly overcome, as happens, by her plight, her sweetness, her helplessness, the ebbing, this dying of the light, such a light, flickering bravely still . . .

~

4

He visited her in her room in the nursing home. Sometimes the six-hundred-and-fifty-mile round trip ended in watching her sleep. At those times he would stay for an hour or so, then go for a walk and a smoke on the beach, hoping she might be awake when he returned.

The home had been built in 1862 as a convalescent home for the wealthy. Its location was designed to take advantage of the healing properties thought to be in the ozone from the sea no more than two hundred yards away. The building sat behind deep defensive lines of sand dunes, lush with spiky marram grass, rivuleted with a network of small half-concealed pathways, haunted by transient bathers, dog-walkers and erotic hideaways.

John never failed to enjoy the building. It had a long frontage, a vaguely Palladian aspect, a bold isolation. It faced what had once been a busy railway line but was now given over to gorse and scrub. It looked every inch a grandiose country house: save that it had only one floor. As if the ground floor had been built and then the money ran out. Was it a failed investment that could hide its shame as it stood half a mile outside the seaside town? Or just another example of privileged eccentricity?

In fact its stunted one-storey height and its extraordinary length – which held more than forty bedrooms, several sitting rooms, kitchen, dining room, offices, storerooms – were deliberate. The wide corridors, the broad walnut doorways, the multitude of long windows were specifically designed for those whose mobility was limited. Even the imitations of grandeur could be seen as healing: who could not feel better, living for a while spoiled in such opulence?

And so they had come to be healed, for more than a hundred and fifty years: the neurasthenic and the broken-limbed, the war wounded and the abandoned, the sick, the

5

broken-hearted, the dying and the diseased. Among those who had sought refuge were John and his mother immediately after the war when it had been a sanatorium for sufferers from tuberculosis: they had been kept in for no more than a couple of weeks.

Now it sheltered the old and the very old, the ill and the terminally ill. Those who could, paid; most did not. Each room had a small bathroom; the staff were local women. These women, through their parents and relatives and friends, knew or felt they knew those they cared for: it was a family of place.

When he read of the neglect of old people in other such homes and heard the stories of cruelty and despair, John thanked his lucky stars. It was lucky, too, that his mother had lived all her life in a small market town a few miles inland and was therefore eligible for the home; and most of all he was grateful for the goodness that could be garnered and cultivated still among local women whose caring job was a job they wanted to do.

Despite the understandable pessimism of the day, when John looked at this home and appreciated the ambition to support the entire population from the cradle to the grave in such an economically straitened island, there was a pride to be taken, he thought, in such a democratic act of decency.

His mother went to sleep and he went out for some air. When he made for the sea he would circumnavigate the great beached home, and trek through the pines to the dunes ankle deep in sand, years deep in the past. He remembered these dunes as superlative cowboy-and-Indian territory on his schoolboy day trips there with his mother and their friends, and later as subtle playgrounds on school trips and choir trips, and still later as disturbing mating grounds when he and his pals biked the ten miles in the hope of a sexual adventure. There

6

had been one eruptive adolescent passion, he remembered (and always would), when a wild girl, teasing, older, who knew the ways of the dunes, had maddened him, possessed him, then dumped him and left him achingly bewildered.

Visits to his mother provoked memories as strong as the surge of the sea that swept over from the Atlantic and around Ireland, and sped into the inlets and crannies, the rivers and estuaries and firths that stabbed into the body of Britain on the west coast. Along these water routes had come the settlers who had given breed and tongue to the county his mother was bound to.

When he was with her it was as if she were the tidal moon pulling up depths from his life thought forgotten, himself the willing sea, ready to race across the sands or be thrown against the rocks, not wanting it to ebb away. He felt this place course through him; this lonely area of the far north-west of England, this county of war and pillage, of unimaginable wealth and poverty alike, this, his England, once a spinning globe of red glory to the boy who had loved it with an innocent, ignorant, imperial passion that still glowed in the ashes of the present.

Across the sword of sea before him, the Solway Firth, he looked towards Scotland with its hill-line mildly matching the more massive and poetic fells of the Lake District a few miles to the south, behind him. At evening time he would, when lucky, catch the gorgeous blaze of sunset to the west, the daily death, the never constant interplay of ever-reshaping clouds, the range of colours, some so pastelly delicate it was impossible to ascribe to them their precise shade, some so lyrical, some magnificently uncompromising – gold, crimson, red; the day, the world ending in a furnace.

Or there would be sullen days, just as compelling, the pressing heaviness of grey-black mountains of bruised clouds, a sea rippled in lead, hills across the water misted and dangerous, the wind whistling up the death wails of armies fatally believing they had the time to march across the temporarily sea-less sand to surprise Scotland, their old enemy, only to be surprised themselves by the speed of the tide as it raced in to embrace the clear border streams. They had drowned, those English warriors, in their thousands. The end of their world in this lifeless landscape. Was her loss of memory a sort of drowning? At night the little fishing boats with their tiny lights were like the lost souls of those armies, still calling for help. Like her broken sentences.

He liked to walk back at dusk to the home with its own tiny lights at a distance. He would always pause for a last cigarette. He hoped he was ready for whatever degree of wakefulness or sleepiness, of anger or love was waiting for him. He was now her pole star. Many years ago he had decided that being the only child made things simple. With his father dead, and despite his children and other relatives and friends and the nurses, he had to be her keystone.

And 'Hello?' she said, this day, questioning as she had done a couple of hours before. He sat beside her. He had about an hour left. She was still half asleep, small even in the modest bed, and puzzled.

'Hello,' he said. He took her mottled hand. It was cold. He rubbed it. 'It's John.'

'John? No, it isn't.'

'It is.'

'You're *not*.'

There was a sorrow but there was a calm also. His task was to take her away from this confused present, to lead her into the past, which could be patched up or made up or truly remembered but above all – safe. Safe, safe, safe and away from the abyss that threatened.

8

'Who am I, then?' He smiled. It was not a false encourage-ment. It suggested a game. That might help take the curse off it.

'Well . . .' She cupped and rested her chin on her left hand and considered him as if he were a dog she were judging in a show. 'Let's see your feet.'

He pushed back his chair and lifted them: black-brogue shod. She scrutinised them. 'They're very big,' she said.

'They're just normal.'

'They're *big*.'

He waited.

'You're a Johnston,' she said, 'that's who you are. You're a Johnston.'

'I'm not.' He knew about the Johnstons.

'You *are*!'

She turned her face into the pillow and he thought that she was set for sleep. But she was sobbing. He leaned over to touch her near-fleshless shoulder through the linen night-gown. She ignored his touch. He pulled up the sheet and the blanket so that she would be warmer. She murmured to herself, so low he could not hear. Then again. He leaned forward. 'I want my mother,' she said.

He heard himself ask, 'Which one?'

She stirred and looked at him – but what did she see?

'My own,' she said. 'My own mother. I want Grace to come and see me. Can you bring her? I want my mother.'

Once more she turned away and put her white head into the white pillow and this time she slept, leaving him with the burden of the request.

Maybe they could share an imagined world now. Maybe his thoughts could become her thoughts. For where was she in that dark place but still drifting forward, like a small boat on a black glass of water? Could he not in some way reach her even there, out of his own darkness? Could he not put together a memory for her? Perhaps he could become her memory. To build it from fragments, or make it up. And most of all bring back Grace. Her own mother.

CHAPTER TWO

It was her least difficult birth. The previous three, now eleven, ten and two, had struggled to get into this world, especially Belle, the last. That had been a unique agony. Ruth had screamed, said Mrs Harrison, a neighbour who could act as a midwife, over that one, Belle, 'screamed to scare the crows'. Only by shoving a clothes peg between her teeth could they mute her. This time the child popped out 'like a pea from a pod,' said Mrs Harrison, and less than an hour into labour. Which was just as well, she added, because Ruth was 'finished. It was as if the little girl had taken all the life out of her.'

Even so, there were a few moments of relief and happiness between the two women as the new child was washed and swaddled and returned to her mother. The other children had been farmed out among the few cottages in the hamlet. The father was working away from home, across the county.

'Market day in Wigton,' said Mrs Harrison. 'I couldn't have a better excuse not to go. Our lass can do it. The walk will do her no harm. She's young.'

Mrs Harrison said later that it was like talking to a ghost. The baby had gurgled to sleep in the crook of her mother's listless arm. The low fire hissed from wet logs. The damp from the walls and the beaten earth of the clay daubin cottage brought a chill into the summer room, which the weak fire could not vanquish.

'She tried so hard,' Mrs Harrison was to say. 'She had that lovely smile still and the thinness of her face made her look even finer. I've never seen such a white skin and that head of black hair. She smiled and she tried to speak but, poor soul . . .'

Outside the one-storey cottage, the like of which would have been there or thereabouts in the Middle Ages, was a country at that time the most powerful on earth. As the British nineteenth century strode through its last few years, and Queen Victoria, monarch of an empire on which the sun never set, welcomed as her prime minister an aristocrat whose direct ancestors had performed much the same duty for Elizabeth I, there was a Himalayan range of prosperity. There was invention, industry, intelligence, variety, philanthropy, progress, genius, style and some charity. And wealth – wealth beaconed in the splendour of fine mansions and rolling acres of private land. A woman like Ruth, who had worked at menial tasks all her life, had she had the energy and not been so firmly schooled in obedience, might have wondered where all the poverty came from. In such oceans of plenty, why did so many still starve? In such ferocity of industry, why did so many seek work and not find it, and so many in work be barely able to sustain life? In such pastures green, why were there so many small graves? In such a noble country, where was the sense of being one noble country together?

Ruth did not ask these questions: Ruth was not part of that. She was proud of her hamlet, she was uncomplaining of a fate that sent her husband, a hardworking farm labourer, scavenging across the county for employment, dossing in ditches, eating slops. She would say that she had had a good life even as now it was slipping away from her so swiftly.

A doctor came from Wigton, a kindly man who would not charge. He saw the high fever, the shaking chill, the rapid breathing, the slackening of sense and speech. He gave what medicine he had in his case, morphine, and advised constant tea and water and knew it was too late for the hospital. The beautifully spoken, well-connected young deacon came and embarrassed himself in the cottage as Mrs Harrison and others and the children watched him in his magisterial black clothes and waited for some sign. But all he felt was this embarrassment at his uselessness among these women of rough tongues and gentle gestures and faith. The other children were called in.

Word was got to both her husband and her father. Wilson, her father, arrived first. He was almost sixty now but the five-mile walk had been rapid. He took both her hands and waited until she was calm and coherent and told her that if it came to it he and her mother would take on the children and they would be looked after. They would always be safe and well fed. Had she heard him? 'Yes,' she whispered. He then sat in a corner, and he folded his arms, and he waited.

When their father came, the children flew to him and clung about him so that for a while he could not move from the low doorway. The choke in his voice as he said his wife's name made Mrs Harrison and the two other neighbours turn away, quelling their tears, wanting the couple to have some privacy.

And the new child gurgled and only occasionally cried as the women cradled her and held her close, shielding her, it seemed, protecting her from the fever of her dying mother.

It was when the candles were guttering in the first light breeze of dawn. It was even before the first birdsong, the fire almost dead. It was at the pitch of half-light that she shuddered out of life gently, as if not wanting to disturb anyone, with the same ease as had brought this sweet woman's last child into the world.

She was a Tuesday's child: 'full of grace', the rhyme said. Grace she would be.

CHAPTER THREE

Mary had been in the home for three years. Assessments were provided regularly. John also made his own.

As he lived so far away, he had been unaware of the slow degrees of the early decline. His visits north in those pre-dementia days were often rushed, robust affairs. Members of his family or himself, or all together, were bent on 'taking Grandma out'. Out of her terraced cottage in a close near the town centre, out of her normal routine, out of herself – into the galloping warmth of their embrace, into outings, times for sensations and exclamations. Reflection and explanation were largely ignored. So, for two or three years, under the static of over-activity, the problem was unsuspected, the occasional misremember-ings or splashes of forgetfulness rather fondly cherished. The stealthy erosion of her defenceless mind passed unno-ticed, and the disease went about its business undisturbed, relentlessly, both the stalker and the reaper.

There were three incidents that significantly signalled the extent of the decline.

John had arrived a couple of days before Christmas. He registered at the last small hotel in the town that took in guests. He had a drink and then wandered through the fairy-lighted streets he could have navigated blindfold, enjoying the familiar seasonal temptations in the small shops. They were empty streets this early in the evening, pavements glittering still from the afternoon downpour. Down a slit of an alley, across a yard, on the path to her cottage and framed in the archway at the end of the path, he saw an agitated woman, looking all about her as if stranded in traffic.

As he walked towards this silhouette she resolved the agitation and walked quickly towards him, towards the fairy-lights of the town, no coat, no scarf, clopping heels on the wet cobblestones. It was his mother. She would have walked past him but he barred her way. Her hair, he could see in one of the few streetlights, was brushed violently to one side. But it was the lipstick, smeared around her mouth, and a high rouge powder coated on her cheeks that sank him.

It was the first time she had not recognised him. He took her back to the cottage, fire full on, every light lit, the dwarf Christmas tree ablaze, the table uncleared. She did not know where she had been going and he did not enquire. He stayed overnight in the spare bedroom.

There were cousins nearby who were devoted to her, and others about the close and in the town, and all of them said, 'We've been noticing for some time but we didn't want to worry you. She was just about managing. We didn't want to bother you.' And what could he say but tell me, worry me, bother me, but that would be a criticism of those who kept a lookout day after day while he turned up only occasionally and rarely for long. So they assured him they would keep a closer eye and tell him everything. It had been a 'one-off' they said, and he let himself be reassured.

But the next night, in the hotel bar, when he left her for half an hour for a cigarette and a Scotch, he could not let it go. Where would she have gone? To a friend? It was not her way to 'drop in' and she was too confused for such a coherent plan. To a pub? She did not drink but what other doors would be open at that time, what lights and fires on, what warmth anywhere else? There would be those who would know her but what would even they make of this old lady blotched for a night out? Who would have taken her home? What would they have made of her, vulnerable, needy, utterly adrift with no self in sight? How had she got into that state of mind and appearance?

He was shaken by her appearance. She was always neat about herself. Yet something of the Dickensian lamplit street, something of the darkness of sordid back alleys, the faintest trace of the gutter courtesan, had transformed her. And there was something, too, of the innocent, an old doll unexpectedly wound up and sent out in unsuitable finery to take her place in a world she would no longer recognise. Who would have taken her home? The town was no longer the intimate network and nest it had been in her childhood and his.

But calm, calm. The town, though gutted since her day, the medieval heart and intense slum cohabitation ripped out of it so that many of Mary's lifelong friends had decamped beyond the boundaries of the old small settlement, would surely still recognise one of its own. Surely, he thought. 'It's Mary,' someone would have said. Somebody who had known her at school or at church. 'Mary. You look a bit lost . . . You look . . .' He wished he could forget that look but he never did. What if the old codes of recognition had broken down as some lamented? He was being over-dramatic. She would have been recognised by friends and returned home. Or she would have met with the kindness of strangers. He had got there first and that was all, that was the

17

blessing of it. But his fear was real and the beginning of an ending rose up from the horizon.

Over the next few months the reports were not encouraging. He cut corners and went north more often.

She liked to go to church for the nine-thirty service on Sunday morning. It was the best attended. A century ago a town of twelve thriving churches, chapels and meeting houses, now four but even so it was an encouragement to the vicar that they could raise more than sixty in the congregation at nine thirty still and put out a choir. Mary liked it that children came and she was disappointed that after the first hymn they disappeared into the vestry for what was no longer called Sunday school. She liked the tea and chat afterwards. She liked to sing. Whether or not she believed as she scanned and sometimes mumbled the Creed, her son did not know and never would: it was too late and it would be too tactless to ask. She liked to be in that place with these people. That was the meaning of it to her. And she liked him to be with her, although there was no clinginess about her, there never had been, not even when she had gone into the home. She was a stoic. 'No complaints,' was her answer whenever anyone at any time asked her how she was. 'No complaints.'

On that morning they walked to the church through the back alleys both of them liked. The new Millennium bells pealed out, though not as loudly as they would have liked because of a handful of objections to 'Sunday noise'. It was not especially cold: Mary was finding it harder to stand the cold. 'Starvation' was her word for cold. 'It's starvation.'

In the nine-thirty choral Eucharist in a High Anglican church there is a deal of standing, then sitting, kneeling, then standing, then sitting ... He saw she was a little tired and whispered that she need not stand up to sing the next hymn. But the organ's introduction was a call to arms and she was on her feet, the well-worn words decanting steadily into the elegant Georgian church. Suddenly she sat down. Her head fell over the back of the pew, her eyes wide open, staring at the ceiling. The singing went on.

John never forgot his inadequacy. He sat down beside her and put his arm around her, lifting her head. He saw no sign of her breathing. He sought the pulse on her wrist and could not find it. There was no pulse? He murmured quietly into her ear – 'Wake up, wake up, it'll be fine' – but there was no response from any part of the face set in its expression of staring.

He did not panic. But ought he to have done? He remembered feeling very awkward, twisted in his seat, the cumbersome black winter coat an impediment as he tried to cradle her head. Was she dead? The church service had petered into silence, the congregation as frozen as his mother.

A young woman clambered over the pews. 'Feel her throat,' she said. She touched it quite firmly and intently. 'There's an ambulance on its way. It was just going out of the town. You're in luck.' His mother had not moved and, as far as he could tell, she had not breathed. Where was the luck? And shouldn't it be more than just 'luck' in a church, in a place on holy ground? Meanwhile, save for the young woman, no one in the church moved. The vicar stood near the altar, still as the cross beside him; the choir, having peeped enough, bent their heads; the congregation, mostly behind him, were as quiet as the valley of death. But some were praying, they told him later. Prayers were being said; it was only right that he should know that.

The paramedics came down the nave with a wheelchair. The ambulance was at the church gate. Emergency procedure was followed. Mary came to, a little, and said, 'Is John here?'

'Yes,' he answered, as they sped through to the infirmary, and he took her hand.

The next morning she was like a little girl in her white hospital nightgown, her hair braided fine, her eyes alight, wanting to know when she could go home, praising the nurses.

What did he really feel about her seeming death there beside him? It had been a little death; at the very least, an intimation. Why was there only a blankness in him? Not even tears. A nothingness? But how can a nothingness happen? There must have been something. He could not fathom it. Perhaps shock could be quiet and silent. And was his reaction governed by the belief that in a church, with music, with no apparent pain, death for a Christian, a prepared death, was one to be wished for? But who on earth would wish for the death of someone they loved?

The third and deciding event was when she fell and fractured a leg. The mend was reasonably successful but even her slight frame found difficulty putting much weight on it. For her first convalescence she went into the crowded local hospital. The wild night cries of distress and the constant klaxoning of emergency calls to an understrength staff frightened her. She was declared fit to leave, and then what? Or then where? How did you make decisions about the end of a life? Now he had to act. He was told that it was impossible to leave her in her own house. The social services declared it not fit for the provision of home care – so she had to move.

There were careful consultations yet when the decision was reached John felt that he had failed. But the chosen nursing home was the best place, everybody said that. John liked it the moment he saw its strange, rather comforting, single-storey solidity. So did his mother as her wheelchair crossed the broad threshold. She had always liked grand houses. She had admired them in magazines and at the cinema; she had fallen on articles about them and smiled at the photographs of the great rooms, the grand furniture, the paintings, the objects and the gardens and the people so well dressed, the men so tall, the women so slim, so smart.

She was quite excited that first time and said, 'Who lives here?'

'You will.' He contemplated her alarm and the lies began. 'Until you can walk properly.'

'And then I'll be back to my own house?'

'Yes.' For an urgent moment he knew he ought to move from London and bring his family to her, to see her through. It was impractical, but what did her remaining life weigh in the scheme of his own needs? What did 'practicality' add up to? Yet he knew he would surrender to it. He had, he thought, joined the new tribe that left the weakest behind.

John felt the other unasked question often on the tip of others' tongues – why did he not bring her to his house in London? It was big enough. He could see her every day there and, much more importantly, she could see him and his family every day. So why not? Why don't you? Why didn't you? The little strokes and stabs of guilt that had crept up throughout the last few years intensified now and he could see himself in the dock. The prosecuting counsel or counsels, surely many of them, waving his past at him and in chorus saying, 'Why don't you take her to your house in London? It's big enough.' Hornets in his head, an incubus on the heart. And no answer but a ledger of sensible calculations where sense and calculation ought to have been thrown out of the window.

But it's true, he would say in the courtroom of the conscience. We as a family are so rarely there in our house.

21

The children are no longer children; they upped and offed years ago. My wife and I skid around London independently and interminably, committees, commitments, entertainment, engagements . . . The house is empty most of the time and usually only occupied when it's late and dark. It would have to be redesigned as a mini-hospital, because now there are complications not only with the leg but also with her heart and a lump, benign as yet but unmistakable on her breast. And how could her relatives and local friends ever see her, three hundred miles south? And how could London nurses know the local gossip or even where Wigton was or had ever been? Bring her to the isolation of my home? Even this home in Silloth, ten miles from her birthplace, could sometimes seem too far away from her own home.

She would say, not insistently, but often enough, 'When am I going back to Wigton? When am I going to my home?' And the seaside place in which she had her room was a place she had come to on flat carts and in buses, on trips and mystery tours all her life: it had been her spa, her escape from reality and work, her holiday. It was a place of pleasure. Was that nothing? When told she was in Silloth she would smile and say, 'I like Silloth.'

The doctors agreed. His relatives agreed. Everybody agreed with John except John. Three years ago now, and most days it worked for her and the decision had been the right decision. Until she said, 'When am I going home?'

~

He had looked at some of the research on Alzheimer's disease, although it seemed that his mother's case was nearer vascular dementia than Alzheimer's.

22

Yet [he read] vascular dementia and Alzheimer's disease often co-exist, especially in older patients with dementia.

The term refers to a group of syndromes caused by different mechanisms all resulting in vascular lesions in the brain ... Vascular lesions can be the result of diffuse cerebrovascular disease or focal lesions or a combination of both. Mind dementia is diagnosed when patients have evidence of Alzheimer's disease and cerebrovascular disease, either clinically or based on neuroimaging evidence of ischemic lesions ...

She had in some degree, although the intensity fluctuated, most symptoms listed in Wikipedia. Problems with recent memory, getting lost in familiar places, walking with rapid or shuffling steps (though she rarely walked more than half a dozen steps at a time and then always assisted), loss of bladder and bowel control, emotional lability, some difficulty following instructions, problems handling money.

But as Eileen, one of the nurses, was fond of saying, there were 'differences of days'. Sometimes there was incessant repetition in her talk but with better drugs that had lessened over the past months. At the same time she slept much more than she had done. Yet when she was awake she could be alert and engaged and funny still, especially when her grandchildren charged in. At times, even, there seemed evidence of some improvement and repair.

John believed that there was a better way for him to help than this mere visiting. At the moment, he would arrive with magazines and biscuits and chocolates and, if she was in her room – and the nurses usually put her there when they knew he was coming – he would read to her from the newspapers. The property prices in the *Cumberland News* alarmed her.

'You have to be a millionaire! That's just terrible!' Or she would catch sight of a headline, once of the violent abuse of a girl-child by her parents: she read it – her eyesight was intact – and pushed the paper aside. 'How can people do that? How can anybody do that? I'm not reading any more.' In her world the bad had to be rejected in order to be lived with. And her own sensitivity to pain, heightened by her childhood, made her raw when presented with the pain of others, especially of children. She was near weeping over that headline and would not be comforted for some time.

But time did pass and new starts were forever being made and he censored her reading from then on.

She wanted the past, he knew that. She wanted to sing. She wanted reminding of names and people and events she had known back then. She wanted detail. It was the detail that brought her most fully to life.

This disease had to be attacked on all fronts, he thought. Neuro-scientists and researchers the world over were working to find out how to meet this invasion. It was as if it had been sent up from the deep to punish the audacity of the human race in so steadily and cleverly increasing its life span. It did seem, to John, akin to the monsters of mythology that appeared from outer darkness to destroy all the men and women they could discover.

There were many ways to fight such monsters. The old way was to take a sword to the dragon's head, or bind it with a spell, or fell it with a magic word. Science now was the magic word and was marshalling its intelligence to tackle this creeping undergrowth, which strangled the roots of thought.

But there were other approaches, he thought, however modest they could seem. There always had been. In myths and stories that still resonated there were always other paths up the fearful mountain.

He would take her back to halt the forward decline. He would try to work out what might absorb her so that she could be immersed in it. Perhaps in these simple ways the unravelled mind could connect again, the disintegrated could reintegrate, the parts could be made whole, the past could restore the present.

Why could he not help reconstruct parts of her memory? Surely that would be a possible cure. In the next generation or so, John thought, you would have much of your life captured on a small disk – photographs, films, sounds, interviews. People could stock up memory banks for old age. They could plan to replace what Nature threatened to take away – as they did in other ways. Meanwhile he could make a start. He could conjure up Grace and slip in slivers from her life. It was Grace she most wanted. But he could also bring back their mid-century town.

On his walks through the town he had passed the Congregational church, sold off now. It was a bold sandstone building a few yards down from the Anglican church, from which it had seceded. John's father had preferred the Congregational church, if pressed. He respected the views of others, but he had no views on religion save that it was not for him.

In the basement of that church was a space in which an occasional blameless night life went on. There were plays on a stage big enough to take the town's silver band; there were socials and suppers and it could be hired by any party for a meeting. Most of all there was dancing. John just had to walk past the church, which stood alone now at the end of a demolished street, Water Street, once the pulsating slum of the town, to tingle at those memories of dancing.

Everybody had wanted to dance and the catalogue of their dances was as long as your arm. In twos, in threes, in fours, in

25

groups and in the whole slam-bang gang of them, there were dances to fit every combination, save one. One alone was never seen but for the random intrusion by the rather unbalanced lady who lived in a fine house nearby. She would be drawn in by the sound of the band now and then and waltz for a while by herself, at the edge of the stage, before departing with dignity. Otherwise, the single dancer was an unknown species in the basement of the Congregational church.

So he decided. He was at the research stage in the next of his series of biographies of medieval figures in English life; other obligations in London could be managed. He would shore up the ruins of her mind with material from a past she loved. He would try to take her back to the time when the three of them, three generations, were almost together, and to a boy sitting at a table with Grace, a woman he would not be allowed to know.

Love was what she needed. But he thought it could be grounded in giving her access to that time in her life when the whole of her existence was in harmony with the place and the society in which she lived. To help her be again as she had been at her finest in the place and time that inhabited her. He wanted that. He would describe it. He would try to give it back to her, and take her there.

CHAPTER FOUR

Wilson and Sarah went to fetch Grace. His big shire horses were not right for the job so Wilson borrowed a horse from his neighbour. Sarah had scrubbed out the old high-sided cart used for anything too heavy to carry by hand. They lashed a short plank across the front to make a seat and left the farm in the hands of Jacob, their eldest son, who had come from his own smaller holding nearby to give them the time.

It was rare that the two of them trotted out along the lanes on a bright summer's morning and, true to character, they made the best of it. Like Wilson, Sarah was approaching her sixties but good stock, frugal living, plain food, constant exertion and, Sarah would add, the will of God had kept her hardy, alert and little affected by the tightening grip and barnacles of age. For Wilson, it was a good opportunity to look over the hedges and into the fields, to assess the size of the herds, the quality of the beef, the quantity of milk in the swollen udders.

At first Sarah picked out the buildings, approving the stone-built farmhouses of which their own was a modest example, frowning at the derelict barns, shaking her head at the hovels. But soon she switched her gaze to the landscape and quietly savoured the unaccustomed liberty, this holiday.

She had a fine view of the mountains that fortressed the lakes to the south. She had visited the Lake District once when she was much younger and still she thought of it as an enchanted land and still she spoke of it with happiness.

Wilson took his time going through Wigton. It was not a market day but the town was still busy and he took advantage of the trip to leave his pocket watch at the jeweller's to be mended. Sarah bought a few sweets for the children and stocked up on the larger quantities of flour, salt, sugar and pepper, which were more expensive in the village. Economy was a creed, austerity a commandment.

Sarah was a true-hearted and faithful member of the Primitive Methodist chapel in their village, which sat on the first shelf above the richly earthed Solway Plain as it began its rise from the sea to the mountains that formed the centre of the county. The community, a few hundred strong, was nearly self-sufficient, as indeed Wilson and Sarah Carrick were, but Wigton was always there for the bigger items – farm implements, saddlery, hardware. The Primitive Methodist chapel was the only place of worship. This was rather unusual in that area and at that time when religious buildings, especially nonconformist chapels, forested the rural landscape. Wilson tried to attend twice on Sundays but when, rarely, he failed to make it, he felt no guilt. He was his own man.

As a boy of twelve, alongside other boys and girls in the village, he had taken a pledge in that chapel that he would never touch alcohol and he had kept his word. 'John Barleycorn is dead,' he sang lustily, in the sing-songs at the chapel youth club. He would smoke a pipe of black twist most evenings and ignore the suggestions of Sarah that it would choke the lot of them and such foul manure was best left outside. He worked steadily every day and did everything that had to be done to keep his small farm productive and clean.

He kept hens and ducks for their eggs and reared two pigs for butchering at the year end. He butchered them himself in a lean-to shed he had built against the barn. The hams hung from the cruel black iron hooks in the kitchen where the fire was rarely allowed to go out. These would meat them through the year. He was a good shot, and rabbits were brought home to provide variety, though he used his gun sparingly. All their vegetables were grown in his garden. The cows provided the milk and so the cheese and the butter. The orchard produced fruit, which was stored or made into jam. The hedgerows were full of herbs that Sarah knew how to employ. It was said of Wilson Carrick that he could spot a nail on a road and find a use for it.

Sarah had been brought up in a large family of girls and their mother had made clothes and repaired clothes and eventually, in the parlour of the cottage, set up what could be called a shop. Sarah herself made most of the clothes her family wore and had the same unspoken pride in it as she had in baking her own bread and scones and cakes.

The boys gathered twigs and fallen boughs throughout the year to stack for the fire, although coal was cheap and Sarah would not stint on a good fire. It paid its way, she said. It warmed the house through and kept off the chill that came in from the sea and the damp from the frequent rain. Cold and wet, she knew, could steadily rot a building or a pair of lungs. The weather was friend and enemy, the daily deciding presence, and it was no good praying about it, she thought. God had better things to do.

What might seem a stern sub-stratum of life gave the Carrick family and others like them a sense of themselves, which they knew was hard-earned. Storms from the Atlantic could test them but they could look after themselves, they believed, and that independence need bow to no one. They were deeply anchored.

Their oldest son was settled on his small farm; the second had joined the Army and was serving in the Ashanti war; one daughter had gone into service on a small manor near the county town of Carlisle, fifteen miles away, and then there had been Ruth. And now Ruth was gone there were her children.

There they were, stood outside the cottage, the two boys, one of them holding Belle by the hand. Mrs Harrison cradled Grace and declared that she didn't want to part with her, that she was good enough to eat. It was a full-sun midday and the cottage seemed picturesque and innocent. A few pieces of furniture and the small heaps of cutlery, kitchenware and bowls were soon shifted into the wagon. Sarah gave Mrs Harrison much of the furniture and Wilson insisted that she took a pound 'for your trouble'. Other children, bare-footed, and more neighbours came to wave them off, handkerchiefs flagging their departure as if they were leaving harbour for a long sea voyage. 'Come back to see us, won't you?' called Mrs Harrison, as the cart drew away.

The boys soon settled: there was always plenty of work on the farm. There was plenty to eat. The school was nearby, just a few minutes' walk. They made new friends. They were well shod and clothed. The chapel was much livelier than their Anglican parish church. Their grandparents were always there for them.

Belle was more difficult. Even as a three-year-old she was already too big. There was something dull in the eyes, something laggard in the movements. The excruciatingly slow and painful birth had perhaps caused her damage, Sarah thought, but no matter, she was willing and biddable. She would need to be more closely looked after than the others.

Grace became their joy. No one could see Grace and not smile. Wilson loved to dandle her on his knee. Later, Sarah could not resist letting her run her finger around the bowl in which she had made the mix for ginger snaps or rock buns, and she laughed when the young child sucked hard at her finger to make sure she got the full goodness of it.

~

This time James said he wanted to talk to Wilson before he saw his children. Wilson took him into the outhouse where he did the carpentry. James tried to come through every fortnight, on a Saturday for convenience, catching a morning train from Whitehaven to Wigton. From there he walked the two miles out to Oulton where Wilson and Sarah lived.

After Ruth's death he had found work in west Cumberland and eventually landed up in the coalfield. Hundreds of small mines, mainly coal but some iron ore, were furnishing a sultan's wealth for the local aristocratic family, who owned the land and all that lay beneath it. They also furnished jobs, by the thousand, mostly claimed by men coming in like James from the near-starvation wages of the countryside. However cheaply thrown up the brick-built miners' homes were, they were sounder than the weeping poverty of clay daubin rural cottages; however hard and dangerous the work, the pay was better. And there was a boldness among some of the men that James admired, a determination to improve their lot in life. He had found his niche.

'Well, then,' said Wilson.

'The work's good,' he said. 'I wish I hadn't been so obstinate about it before. Most of the men are good men. Some bastards – sorry, but . . . Money's steady.' He offered Wilson

31

a cigarette even though he knew it would be refused. James was a whipcord of a man, Irish-blue eyes, anger rarely too far away from him, but the sense, mostly, to douse it before it fired. He took a deep pull on the cigarette.

'I told you I'd got lodgings. She lost her man, there was some compensation but very little. There are two girls . . . Well, Wilson, I've asked her to marry me and she's agreed. It'll be very quiet.'

'If you're both suited . . .'

'We are. Well enough.'

'I'm pleased for you. So will Sarah be. It's not good for a man to be alone.'

'I wondered about the boys . . . Belle's too . . . young, and Grace? Still a baby . . .'

'*You* have to tell the boys,' said Wilson. 'They're your sons and they're getting to be men now.' He saw James's hesitation. 'Sarah can be with you when you do it.'

'Shall I ask them to the wedding?'

Wilson paused. 'Do you want to . . . ?'

'The beggar is, I do and I don't.'

'What about your new wife?'

'I think she'd be for it . . .' James dropped the cigarette to the floor and ground it out with the heel of his boot. He kept his head down. 'I think she'd want to keep them.'

'Why not? You'd all be together. Belle and Grace could stay with us.'

'I've seen them here.' James was unmistakably relieved. His new wife did not want the girls. He said, sadly, eagerly, 'They're very settled here.' He searched the older man's face for permission to leave them behind.

'It's not easy for you, is it? . . .' said Wilson. 'You're a good man, James. Whatever you do will be right. You take your time.' They shook hands with an uncharacteristic formality.

The boys went to the wedding, travelling unaccompanied on the train. They stayed overnight and came back fizzing with chatter about the great city, the fires at the pit heads, the black-faced men in the streets, the crowded harbour, the warren of lanes, the size of it ... Later in the year, James, the eldest, went to live with his father and soon found work in the mines as a pony-boy. Tom was to try it for a few weeks but came back to the country and went to work on his uncle's farm.

When Grace reached her fifth birthday, there were only four of them in the house and she was already, her grandfather said indulgently, 'wild as any creature'. She started school, for which on her first day she wore her new red clogs.

CHAPTER FIVE

The boy and his mother set off just after seven on a winter evening that suited the look and the mood of the post-war town. Three years after the victory over Germany, the town remained immured and frozen in the consequences of that mid-century maelstrom. Though the blackout blinds had been removed it still seemed like blackout. The council-house yard in which they lived was pitch and they needed the small torch. The streets were ill lit by gas lamps at thrifty intervals, the pools of dark predominating on the windows of the locked and bolted shops. Above them, in the flats, the owners showed their presence by the dim yellow glow of gaslight through the curtains. The fragile little globes of the mantles plopped into a feeble flame all over the town and yet the impression was of overwhelming darkness, the gas subdued as if in sorrow.

They walked quickly. Mary, a bonny young woman in her late twenties, the luxuriant black hair, the fine skin, the body lean from work and the prescriptive diet of rationing. The boy aged eight, in short pants, allowed his Sunday suit for this occasion, hair plastered flat with water and a stiff comb, grey socks up to the knees, shoes shining. He was excited and Mary had to step out to keep up with him.

The lure was the hand-painted poster stuck outside the

Spanish fish-and-chip shop alongside the much bigger poster advertising the three films coming to the Palace Cinema that week. It read 'Pea and Pie Supper – bring your own knife and fork. Proceeds to the Social Fund. Adults one shilling. Children and others threepence. Dancing to the "Two Wigton Mashers". All welcome at the Wigton Congregational Church Hall. 7.00 p.m. Tuesday 10th.'

Like the prey to a hawk, like the fox scent to a hound, this poster, once John had confirmed that his mother would take him to it, inflamed the small boy's desire. 'Dancing'! And out late! With a band! Few aristocratic private parties or courtly levées or gatherings of swells in legendary hotels or the massed horsy packs at county hunt balls had been as passionately anticipated as this. With a Pea and Pie Supper thrown in! His mother let him carry the knives and forks.

They went up Water Street, only lately cleared of the tuberculosis epidemic that had crept through its damp congested slum of dwellings. Council rehousing was under way, with the radical luxury of indoor bathrooms, spacious bedrooms and gardens; it was a dramatic transformation. Even so there were tears in the eyes of the Water Street crowd and a persistent regret among the older ones that this slum was to be erased. It was a sewer of disease, this street that had been proudly theirs, but it had also been a pump of life, a place of intense neighbourliness in the centre of the town, with its cow-cack-splattered road as the cattle were herded down to station on market day, with its screaming pig auction and its fearful reputation. Even Mary, who 'liked the people but not the street' felt, on this cold evening, the draining away of something she could not articulate, some ancient spirit of survival gone, a dauntless people . . . Half evacuated, Water Street looked touchingly romantic in the gaslight.

The Congregational church was at the end of the street and Mary saw two shadows turning to go down the steps to the basement. Other members of the committee, early as she was, to help out. While they set up the trestle tables and heated the food, John and two other children chalked the floor and made slides and skidded on it on dusters to make it fit for dancing.

The women talked ceaselessly as they laid the table, walking to and fro. A two-bar electric fire made a doomed attempt to warm the room. Most of the women kept on their coats; only a few removed their hats. Generally they were better spoken than their men, especially in public. John, and all his friends, liked to hear and speak their own Wigton dialect, seamed, though at the time he did not know it, with Old Norse and Anglo-Saxon and Romany but all of it claimed as 'Wigton' by those in the town who prided themselves that their own patter was 'a language that the strangers do not know'. Later, long after he had left the town, he could still call up those old words, a warm history on his mid-century tongue, now banished to self-conscious silence.

'Laal' was little, 'gaan yam', going home, 'laik' was play, 'beck' was stream; in their hundreds the Celtic and Norse words strode out in a much-loved march from the past. There was the biblical 'thee and thine', Romany 'chavvas and morts' and words brought back like presents by men who had served in India: 'parnee' for rain, 'gadji' for man. It was the common tongue in the rougher part of town, stigmatised as vulgar by outsiders and those who thought they were above it or feared its taint. It was a language of the included. It was tribal, a proud mark of difference: theirs; and his. Then.

The men had now arrived. Every man wore a suit, often the same style as those made in Savile Row, and something of the same cut. Tight ties, polished shoes, hair usually stiffened into obedience by Brylcreem. Most of them would have served in the war or done their two years of National Service in a vast armed force that still considered itself the policeman of an empire that was beginning to break apart. Drill, combat, order, orders and military consciousness were in the men. Even here at the Pea and Pie Supper. It was as if scenes like these were the final salutes to the wounding adventure of a world-wide empire governed by a small island located, as an early pope had said 'at the uttermost end of the earth'.

And yet, on that night at this Pea and Pie Supper, there was perhaps a moment before the world turned. The British, they thought – when they gave it a thought, which was not often – had won. In that bleak, cold basement they didn't talk about it but it was in them. They had shown who they were. They had shown what they were made of. They had stood up for what they thought was right against a Great Evil when the Russians had joined the Nazis, when France had been overrun and surrendered and much of the rest of Europe had either sided with the Fascists or backed off, when the Americans had stood aside and Hitler was set to snuff out everything that was in his way.

They alone, and for a time crucially, had stood up to the evil bullies. The skill and courage of the pilots, the intrepid expense of treasure, had held the bridge. Others had piled in afterwards, and the British part had diminished, but when it mattered most it was just them – them alone – the British or, as some would think at the time, the English.

So in that wintry austerity was a stubborn will; in the small commons and deprivation, independence. When the trestle tables were cleared away and the last plate washed, hearts could be whole again, better for the victory and better still for for treating it modestly.

Dancing was announced.

Mr Ismay did the honours. Mr Ismay worked in the accountant's office at the factory. He lodged in a house in Church Street. He was a bachelor and a Temperance man, unmatched, it was locally thought, in all the county in his ability to organise any 'do' or, once organised, 'get things going'. He was the master of the town's ceremonies. You knew it had begun when Johnnie Ismay stood on the platform, clapped his hands for silence, got it, thanked all who had to be thanked – never forgot a name – and commanded everyone to have a good time. He always wore a pin-stripe three-piece suit and a stiff detachable white collar. He parted his brilliantined black hair down the middle, exposing an undeviating thin white line of skin. There were those who said he could have been prime minister.

John knew that for dancing he had to look at the Studholme boys and copy them. Queenie's boys. There were only three of them there that night, one in his last year at school, one well into his apprenticeship, the other on leave from his National Service. All suited. Queenie never took off her coat. Her husband, a machinist at the factory, rarely came along. He was a pigeon man and he pottered about in his allotment at all hours.

Mary loved watching those boys dance. Dancing defined them. They wanted to be Fred Astaire. They bounded lightly through Three Drops of Brandy and the Dashing White Sergeant, setting John an example and giving him tips. They whirled and whooped the Gay Gordons round the room, which was losing the final pockets of its chilly gloom and warming by the minute with the rising body heat. The Canadian Three Step and the Military Two Step rattled along with parade-ground finesse and the room was alive with the joy of it.

You went across the room for your partner after Mr Ismay announced the dance – say, the St Bernard's Waltz. You said, 'May I have this dance?' or even 'the pleasure of this dance'. The woman or the girl always said yes and you went on to the floor together and waited for the band to strike up. After the final chord you escorted your partner back to her seat and said, 'Thank you very much,' or God help you.

John liked dancing with his mother well enough but she kept him right a bit too strictly while other women and especially the girls would encourage him to give it more vim. There were three girls just a bit older than him there that night. He partnered all three and fell for one, though he knew and mourned in advance that she was too old for him. When with the girls he would snatch a glance at his mother, to see her chatting to her partner, or smiling, laughing – glamorous, he thought, dead smart.

She would remember such dances when they talked years later in the home. And most of all she remembered the band and dancing the Valeta.

The band, the Two Wigton Mashers, took its name from a song of the town buried in the pubs of antiquity. It echoed the Victorian music halls and had to be sung by two men, preferably a little tight but essentially men of a certain age who had style.

> Oh we are the two Wigton mashers
> We often go out on the mash
> We wear our tall hats
> We've no shirts on our backs
> And it's seldom we have any cash . . .
>
> We've only just turned fifty-seven
> But we're handsome, light-hearted and bold

Singing 'tra-la-la-la-la'
As we walk down the street
For pride and perfection we never can be beat
The ladies declare that we are a treat
The two Wigton mashers from down Water Street.

Oh we dance and we sing
And we don't care a jot
We're a jolly fine lot
We're all right, when we're tight
And we're jolly good company . . .

There were several jaunty, self-mocking verses. Tommy Jackson, the drummer, part of a big family in the town, a family that crowded into a minute cottage in one of the yards that pocked the place, had seen the commercial possibilities in the title. He not only played the drums, he also did the posters for the Picture Palace; thirteen a week, each one hand-painted in appropriate colours. He washed windows, worked at the sawmill, smoked like a stove and read up on local history. He had been a conscientious objector and sent to the mines for the duration of the war. He provided a good beat.

The melody and the drama was delivered by Fred Ingrams, a six-foot-two ginger-haired former guardsman from down south who had come to Wigton to find work. He had been a bandsman, and could he play the trumpet! Double fingering, triple fingering, any tune you wanted he would catch in a moment and off he'd go, the trumpet calling out to the troops, summoning the game and the lame, its brass perfection ringing with magisterial exhilaration in the heads of the lucky dancers.

John knew even then that his mother liked the Valeta best.

The way it was done in Wigton followed, it was thought, the old Spanish method. Couples circled the room with men in the inner circle, their backs to the centre, and women in the outside circle facing them. The men stepped to the side with their left foot, the women to the right with their right foot; they then stepped back and swung the other leg across and repeated it and repeated again until the music changed and they offered their arms to the partner opposite. Then they waltzed around the room twice until the circle formed again.

For Mary, John would come to think, the glory was the communion of the two circles, and its imitative, gentle parody of distant, unattainable privilege taken over here by ordinary people and made into their own with a smile at the ease of it.

These working men unselfconsciously put hand on hip and swung their legs in an elegant arc as if showing off a well-bred leg. The women, some still in their coats, were mirrored in them and held hands with each other as did the men. They were linked, all together, all equal, all now sharing the restrained high style, the distinction of those born to such displays. Something inexpressible in Mary was made deeply happy by this simple circling, hands held, the perfect form, the globe, the common bond.

Then they would break into twos for the Waltz. Triple time. John had read later that the Viennese Waltz, which lay behind the Valeta, had swept into Europe in a musical and erotic frenzy. The first performance of the Waltz had been encored eighteen times. The youth at the courtly ballrooms of the Hapsburg Empire could not believe the sexual power of the musical rhapsody conjured up by the Strauss family, the furious gliding whirl of the dance itself, a dervish of movement to a severe geometric pattern, but primitive in its call. He saw the dance as the first Viennese unleashing of the unconscious.

For the first time in accepted mass public display, men could press themselves against women's breasts, women feel the thighs of the young bucks who seized them by the waist. And better! The Church was scandalised and set about banning it. Parents were shocked but envious and soon broke ranks. The madness of formal music ripped up the old manners of formal dancing. Wigton had caught this cultural epidemic and danced with a spin, a speed and a style to outgun all the hussars in the Hapsburg Empire.

The Valeta would always be at the end of the evening, at about nine. Outside were the remains of the dead. In that small town alone a long list had been added to the First World War memorial. But in the dance were new seeds now, ready. Promises of a new world, even of a paradise on earth.

Johnnie Ismay made the announcement: 'Ladies and gentlemen, the Valeta.' He stressed the last two syllables. The *e* was drawn out as long as he could stretch it, giving it the full flavour of its foreignness, Johnnie thought, while the 'ta' snapped a command, like a click of the heels *Valeee-ta*! Begin!

The circles formed on the floor. Everybody was on their feet. Fred Ingrams picked up his trumpet and wetted his lips. Tommy Jackson nodded.

And they danced, this dance appropriated from the chandelier-slung ballrooms and gilded courts of Europe. Here in the bare Congregational Hall in Water Street, England, they danced. And how well and passionately they danced! Formal, at first not missing a beat, then with their hearts pounding, free spirits, soaring through just being there, that night, together – being what they were. Unbridled, they danced the Valeta!

Afterwards they stood calmly unmoving and sang 'God Save the King'.

CHAPTER SIX

'I liked Tommy Jackson. He was a conscientious objector,' said Mary, as if he had not told her as much a few minutes before. But this was what he wanted. He put his notes on the bedside table.

'There were some of the men very nasty with him. They could be very nasty, some of them. He was only a little fella. None of the Jacksons were big. I was in the same class as one of his sisters. Elsie had far too many ... A lot of them did then ... There wasn't enough food to go round ... They had to go without many a time ...'

She leaned back on the propped-up pillows and gazed at the ceiling and dozed. John had to restrain himself from applause. Early days but maybe it was working ... He waited. He had learned to school his impatience. It was curious that whereas in London he was often full of agitation, which marred the activity, here he found patience. Time was increasingly precious. He could wholly appreciate now the words of those poets who wrote of Time with such awe and helpless sadness. Underlying everything was the pendulum, steady as sunrise-sunset, every day a counted loss ... so why was there this ease, this calm, this new sense between them sometimes in his mother's small bedroom, why this impressive non-pressure of time? He let her doze a while.

But the value of such a moment made it too good to squander. The quest now was not only to find the truth in a grain of sand but to see all of life in the moment, even in its going, in its rapid downward stream through the hour-glass.

'Queenie Studholme seemed to rule the roost at those dances,' he said.

She came back to the present.

'Queenie did. She ruled the roost. Some of her boys went to Australia. They were all good dancers you know, her boys . . . and she turned them out smart.'

Already she was tiring but perhaps he could keep it in play just a little longer. Why? Was this her form of a crossword? The nearest he could bring her to be more of herself? How could he really know? Yet he wanted to drag it out.

'Everybody said that Johnnie Ismay was a good man at running things.'

'When am I going home?'

He braced himself for the lies to come. 'When you're well enough.'

'I want to go back to my own house.'

It had been sold.

'It's still there whenever you're ready.'

'Is it still there?'

She looked at him as he remembered her look from the beginning of their life together. The look said: Are you telling the truth? The look said: I don't believe you are telling the truth. The look said: Tell the truth.

John felt the childhood panic in his throat. But he was older now: he could lie better.

'When you can walk properly. When they get you walking. You have to stay here until they get that all sorted out. Then you can go.'

She forced him to hold her look just for another moment

or so but the pure searching skewered him. She saw that and turned away.

He made a final attempt: 'Do you remember when we all joined hands and danced the Valeta?'

'Does nobody want me?' she said, still turned away, and then she turned back to look straight at him. 'Does nobody want me?'

~

The county that had nurtured the daffodils famously celebrated in Wordsworth's poem had taken up daffodils as a tourist attraction. They were planted in tens of hundreds of thousands alongside the motorways, on the run in to the towns and villages that had close connections with the poet. They were by the lakes, beneath the trees, and in every spare bed in every Cumbrian municipal garden.

The public turned official policy into a private craze and the bulbs were scattered in hedgerows and woodland, at the rim of fields and down farm lanes, in private gardens and window boxes and lavishly in cemeteries.

Mary was ecstatic about daffodils. They besieged the home. They filled the vases in her bedroom and in the communal sitting room. They filled her with a delight that John could scarcely fathom, only observe and feel her pleasure smile deeply on him. And, having wrapped her up almost to mummification, he took her out in the car, daffodil hunting.

There was never far to go. He pointed the car down the coast road and slipped into the medieval fortified villages, which now basked in the riches of the Solway farmland, and there they found daffodils in multitudes, as if the sea had

47

swept in across the beaches and deposited a golden harvest of its own to add to the celebration.

They went on the main road to Wigton, which was massed with daffodils on either side, rank on rank like an imperial army on parade, row on deep row, the green and the yellow, swinging in the breeze under the long, high sandstone walls of the railway station, on parade to receive the inspectors in motor-cars who sped past like royalty taking the salute.

He took her beside the nearest park, and up to the foot-hills of the northern fells and into those embedded hill villages alongside the streams and the waterfalls where, quite suddenly and surprisingly clustered on a verge or on the back of a ditch, clutches of daffodils grew under those racing clouds as if they had been poured down from the sky itself, showered golden on the bare fell lands, radiant for those spring weeks, laughing at the slate bleakness of the place, trumpeting happiness.

And everywhere Mary went in wonder. 'Oh, look!' she said. 'Oh, look at them! Aren't they beautiful? Look how many! And more! Aren't they just beautiful?' John drove carefully and slowly and often he would turn and drive back so that she could see again, be utterly absorbed again and exclaim in rapture again and be taken out of herself by the beauty of the daffodils.

~

Sometimes when she was fast asleep, curled up in the bed, her face grave and even severe, he would hear the words of a song. 'Where do you go to my lovely, when you're alone in your bed? Would you tell me the thoughts that surround you, I want to look inside your head.'

Where did she go? Was he watching the closing down of a machine? Long service, worn out, resisting in parts, in others broken and frayed, silted up, chokingly webbed in the intricate threads of ageing, a Gulliver tied down by hundreds of Lilliputians, a body less and less fit for the physical purpose of life, waiting for the final mechanical failure?

And was this sleep a dreamless deadness? She never mentioned her dreams. She never talked of a nightmare. Was she lucky in that or did the forgetfulness strike so deeply that the unconscious regurgitation of the day which flashed up on the screens of sleep was also beyond memory? But did they occur? Soon the neuro-scientists would know. Perhaps they did already. A machine would have been invented that could measure and image the nightmare as it happened, if it happened. Why was it painful not to know it was happening? Because it could mean she had lost a substantial part of being human?

Or was there something outside the machine, once held to be true, and for so long, by so many of genius and understanding: a spirit, a soul? John wanted there to be a mind as well as a brain, a spirit as well as a substance – something *other*. Just as he wanted there to be free will despite the battalions of researchers advancing remorselessly to demolish that essential human craving. All life would be explained, he had read, by chemistry. John admired the truth-seeking of such people. He just wondered, was that the sum of it? Astonishing, given the attacks on 'the soul' over the last two hundred years and given his own scepticism, there was still this niggle that said: But is that all? Can we be sure we are on the road to knowing everything?

It was puzzling to have such a magnificent, even freakish, physical entity as the brain – with more movements in the synapses than atoms in the universe, with a memory store now, through its technological servants, reaching galactic proportions, an intelligence building more intelligence. But with no purpose . . . ? A brain as much a miracle of accidental development as the earth itself. A brain built to survive on the savannah, and now just a few thousand years later able to probe deep space inside and outside the mind itself. Innate curiosity was solving old mysteries by the day and turning them into new marvels, which soon became commonplace. Was that not enough? Should 'the other', the soul, not be let fall away like the launching capsule of a space rocket?

When he thought about this, John acknowledged that he still trailed behind him stories from his past and the past he had studied in his past. He recognised the force of reason and, like so many others, he had reasoned away God in his adolescence. A personal God? How vain and impossible to think that. An all-powerful God? Meaningless or mad. A God of goodness? Look around. A resurrection? Matter forbade it.

And yet, John thought, despite this new supreme being of reason, John felt there was a lingering. Perhaps only a tribal lingering in the silence of an empty parish church or in Choral Evensong and even in the arcane practices of Christian services with the bowings and vowings, the Holy Spirit and the miracles. So weird and yet so passionate and complex, he thought, and perhaps – who knows? – pointing light into that mass of dark matter in our minds and in the universe itself.

Could faith not stand for, not mean, but represent, something that might later in the human story be uncovered? Might its almost bizarre claims not hint at intimations outside our present ability to know, worlds that might exist when we knew more? Or perhaps we were on the way to creating new 'humans' who would be the children of a physics that would know what we could never understand.

Could religion's purpose have been to attempt to locate the inexplicable, of what we could never really know but only feel in pulses, hints, fleeting, speechless patches of thought?

Besides, was reason the only instrument of understanding? David Hume, a philosopher John thought superior to all the current atheistic rationalists, had written that reason responded to and ordered the passions in ourselves, the sensations, the feelings, the thoughts that lay too deep for tears, the heart with its reasons reason did not know. Reason was not a primary but a secondary organ of understanding. Was that right? If so, what followed?

For if there was that 'other', did this all but inert small body tucked up in bed in front of him know about that? She had been transported by the daffodils; others were by music, by painting, by art, by sex, by the power of sensations . . . Was that accounted for in the rational mechanical scheme of things? Perhaps, soon, it would be. And the magic of a real nightingale would then be seen by all as in a higher league than the magic of any imagined nightingale.

Yet it was imagination that was at the crux of it, of what we are, he thought. An imagination that could contain a God but was not a God: an imagination that could conjure goodness and yet not be good, see and even provoke evil but not itself be evil, entertain the brutality and the beauty of every religion and know that the wickedness that came from religion was not in the idea of religion itself but in the primal lust, which is for power. Maybe imagination was religion. Religion was neither good nor bad but people made it so. Yet what did we know of the imagination, which could take us back to the Big Bang faster than the speed of light, which meant one could 'be' other people in the empathy of life or theatre or fiction, which it seemed could

51

do the most impossible thing of all: make something out of nothing.

When asked what was most important for his work, Einstein had answered, 'Imagination, above all, Imagination.' And Shakespeare wrote that poets conjured words out of 'the thin air' and gave them 'a local habitation and a name'.

Their words had inspired and reassured John in his own work as a biographer. Now, before him, was someone whose life was present but whose life history appeared to be crumbling and fading away. Was there life and identity without a history? Was her plunge away from the world he lived in a dying? Or could it possibly be a plunge back down into the black seabed where the oldest creatures still lived and had lived for millions of years without light, without heat, without changing? Or was he watching a complex of particles about to turn back to other particles – of dust? But, then, might not those particles reassemble in time, not as her, not as this all around them, but as another expression of life?

Almost calmly he found he wanted that. He wanted there to be an ending for her better than just a finish. Or was that merely love?

He took up his book and waited to see if she would wake while he had time.

CHAPTER SEVEN

Wilson watched her. He could not help himself. Grace had come in towards the end of his unwinding life like a blessing. But even as he thought that, he smiled, for she was as much an imp as an angel and he was not sure that it was not the dangerous imp that beguiled him.

He watched her. She needed watching. He watched over her. And she knew, the imp, that she had his eye and now and then she would flick him a glance or a special smile and he would find himself smiling back at her for no reason but that she was so alive to him. And she learned, the angel in her, that she had to take care of his feelings towards her, not to trespass too far, not to worry him too much, to watch herself.

Yet he went about his work, dawn to dusk, as gravely as ever, leaving nothing half done, nothing unchecked, nothing to chance. He had two hired men, in their twenties; one lived in the attic, the other went back to his neighbouring home. They went about their tasks under Wilson's ordering. They considered themselves fortunate, though the work was hard, the hours long, the weather often punishing, strength-sapping even for young men. But the food was plentiful and even varied. The house was kept warm. Sarah Carrick made sure their clothes were dried out. The religion was present but not oppressive. It was a calm, rather quiet place, which emphasised all the more the sweet outpourings of the little songbird that was Grace.

Belle was spellbound by her younger sister. The doctor could find 'nothing wrong' with Belle, he said. The understanding of thyroid deficiency was some distance in the future. And so there was a tendency to think that Belle's size, her calf-yearning brown eyes, her slowness, her rather simpleness was her own fault. Or, if you were as dyed in the Lord as Sarah Carrick, an act of God that could not be fathomed by poor human guesswork. Sarah had decided that Belle was blessed. Grace, she thought, had been allocated many gifts. The blessing was on Belle. In her simplicity Belle saw all life as good. In her slowness she was reluctant to cast blame on another; in her obedient harmlessness she was a lesson in sweetness. And so Sarah protected Belle and saw that she was helped. And she feared for her. What would she do, she often thought, after my time?

But the Carricks showed no sign of yielding to the biblical injunction that three score years and ten was the span of life. They went on going on, through their sixties, into their seventies, with little obvious yielding to time. Wilson's fingers were bending over more stiffly to the force of arthritis. Sarah was just beginning to forget things – but by faith and by work they prospered.

They were among the elders in their chapel, and the minister visited them at least once a week. Mr Walker chose his time carefully. At high tea on a Saturday when the work day ended earlier, there was a sense of ease, time for talk and, as the young man openly admitted, it was the best time to have 'a good feed'. Sarah made sure of that. Mr Walker was too thin, she thought, failed to take proper care of himself in the dismal, damp little cottage the congregation provided for him and, as a bachelor, would have no knowledge of or aptitude for cooking. Great Saturday helpings assaulted his bony frame and it shuddered at the impact of the meats, the cold potatoes, the bread, the cakes, the cheese. Nor could he set off home without a parcel 'for tomorrow'. His lean salary was fattened by such gifts in kind around the village.

When the tea was done and the table cleared, Wilson liked to cut off a slice of black twist, invite Mr Walker to take the chair opposite his own across the fire, and talk. Wilson was firm in what he knew and just as certain about what he did not know. He regarded Mr Walker as his weekly education.

Mr Walker took *The Times* and read it carefully. He excused the expense on the grounds that he found it useful for his sermons. It was also, he thought, important for his congregation, which could be wholly immersed in a world easily boundaried by an afternoon's stroll. And when he spoke of foreign wars and foreign continents, of the House of Lords and the Parliament at Westminster, of Great Debates and Great Issues of the day, he was bringing them news of their day on the back of which he could more tellingly bring the eternal Good News itself.

Wilson Carrick wanted more. He had a taste for abstract discussion. He wanted to know how the world had become as it was and why and in all particulars, and both he and the minister would manoeuvre the conversation in that direction. On this Saturday, after some unproductive passes, Mr Walker brought up a subject that he knew would hook the interest of his host.

'Grace is quite outstanding in the Sunday school,' he said.

Wilson fought down his pride just as he checked any sign of it in Grace herself. But this was milk and honey. This was manna. So he said nothing.

'What is she now, ten?' the minister continued. 'Yet she'll pull me up if she thinks I'm wrong.'

Wilson glowed but a deep pull on the black twist would have to do for his reaction.

'Miss Errington says it's much the same at school. She's had to put her up one class above her age already and she could go further.'

'She mustn't be let do that,' said Wilson. 'It will do her no good. One class higher than she should be is more than enough.'

'I'm not sure that I agree. Remember how Christ himself was praised by the elders in the Temple when he was only a boy.'

Wilson shook his head. He knew the passage but the suggestion of a comparison was not comfortable.

'I only say that when we see a gift we should be glad and encourage that gift.'

'Not if it means she gets above herself,' said Wilson, and blew out a plume of black smoke.

'Should we not aspire to be above ourselves? Is that not the burden of the Message? To cast aside what keeps us low and full of sin and look up, reach up . . . ?'

'Not,' said Wilson, unsure of himself, 'if we lose ourselves.'

'But isn't losing yourself, the Self, and becoming part of the body of Jesus Christ, what we are instructed to do? Don't we see a Oneness in all things, that all things were made by Him and everything comes from the same seed, all that lives and breathes and exists comes from the One origin? And do we not seek to understand that mission in our own lives and join it in our second death?'

'You're a bit beyond me there, Mr Walker. I was talking about Grace, a child that needs to be watched.' He paused. 'What second death?'

'We are dead before we are born,' said the young man, who could find in his sermons and even in such a

56

conversation as this an outlet for the passion that had as yet found no expression or fulfilment in love. 'We need to remember that.'

'What good would it do us? If you don't mind me asking.'

'All knowledge is good.'

'Is it?' Wilson leaped in. 'Didn't the Knowledge of Good and Evil set off the whole business on the wrong track in the first place? Doesn't that mean there's things better left alone?'

'I don't believe so . . . It is too important a question to answer lightly, Mr Carrick. I'll think about it and perhaps I'll preach on it when I have found an answer . . .'

Wilson felt relieved, though he was not clear why.

He waited for more.

~

Grace was expected to help in the house and by example learn how to run a careful household. Her accomplishments were a cross between those of a medieval princess and a domestic servant. She could sew with a fine skill; she could knit in wool and make lace; she could embroider. She liked to sing and was encouraged, to draw and she was admired. In the kitchen she peeled potatoes, scraped carrots, chopped up cauliflower, boiled beetroots, cooked, baked and had no squeamish feelings when she helped her grandmother skin and gut a rabbit. She laid the table and served at it, helped wash up the dishes and scrub the pans.

On the farm itself she was given a more marginal role, which she regretted. She liked to see the slow walk of the dreamy cows to the byre for milking and was sure she could have milked if they had let her but her grandfather forbade it. He would sit her on one of the shire horses now and then for a treat but there was no suggestion of a pony. Belle and herself were given half a dozen banty hens each and they fenced in the cheeky miniatures and scattered food for them in the morning and evening and collected the tiny eggs. When they were older he gave them each a lamb every spring, and they would lie in bed after saying their prayers, sunk in the goosefeather mattress in that opulent drowsing of the moment before sleep, primed with cosiness and the warmth of each other and the thought of their worldly treasures, the lambs and the banty hens.

~

With her fourteenth birthday and the end of her school days in view, Grace had become Miss Errington's assistant in everything but official recognition. In the two-roomed school, which housed just over forty pupils between the ages of five and fourteen, she helped to teach the youngest to read, sometimes read stories to Class One and took the singing lessons.

Miss Errington had slowed down quite noticeably and there was concern about her in the village. She dismissed any talk of illness or retirement and let it be known that she was determined to soldier on. But would she be allowed to? The whisper went around until it reached the schoolmistress herself and she was afraid. If only Grace could be trained up as a pupil-teacher, that would give her more time. Time to prepare herself, to look around, to see how she could stretch her small savings and the mean pension to be paid to her only when she reached retirement age, still six years on.

Scheming was foreign to Miss Errington. She had many qualities and skills but cunning plotting to secure something for herself was not one of them. She called on Sarah and Wilson on a Sunday afternoon. She had told Grace what she intended to say to her grandparents. Grace, doubtful and confused by the flattery it implied, said she would take good care to be out.

That was the first time Miss Errington had been inside the farm and she felt enwombed by its warmth, its devotion to hard work, its oak-beamed, polished welcome. It was difficult for her to be the person they so much respected when she felt rather minimalised by the rooted couple sat side by side across from her, expectant.

But first there was the tea with scones; the cake could await the outcome. Miss Errington had prepared her case.

'I'm sure you know from her marks that Grace is doing exceptionally well at school.' Sarah smiled but more to help the schoolteacher along than to join in any praise. Wilson waited and merely nodded when she concluded her report.

'I think she has potential,' she said. 'I point her to books, to *Jane Eyre* and *Silas Marner* and *The Mill on the Floss*, which I thought might be a little beyond her, but she gobbled them up and more, even *Wuthering Heights* and the whole of *Oliver Twist*. They are only novels, I know, but there is poetry too, Lord Tennyson and Sir Walter Scott and some Wordsworth. They are all full of information and fine observations and she races through them – and others – and when there is nothing new available, she reads them over again. It has given her a broad mind, I think. It has given her influence on other minds. And the teaching help she gives me has proved she has a knack for it . . .' Both Sarah and Wilson were intent now, caught in the force of this wholly unforeseen development. 'If you would be willing, I would like to try to arrange for her to stay on at the school and become a pupil-teacher. I would supervise her for the duration of the apprenticeship, for that is what it would be. And after that, who knows where it could take her?'

'Have you talked to Grace about this?' Wilson asked.

'I raised it with her.'

'What did she say?'

'She said I would have to talk to you.'

'Did she take to the idea?'

'I think so. But she can speak better for herself.'

'Would it be costly?' Sarah asked the question she knew that Wilson wanted answering.

'I thought – if it proceeds – to ask Mr Walker about that.'

'But we can't expect it to be done for nothing,' said Wilson.

'I doubt it.' Miss Errington was firm as she always was when answering difficult questions.

'It'll take some thinking about,' Sarah said, 'that's for sure.'

'I appreciate your faith in the girl and your care for her best interests,' said Wilson.

The farmhouse kitchen was silent. The dwindling winter afternoon gave up the struggle and slid towards the dark. For a few minutes the three of them sat in silence, wondering.

~

The compound of excitement and dread on her visits was uncomfortable and Grace never got used to it. But as the train drew into Whitehaven Station after its trek through the severe industrial coastline, with the slagheaps, the pit heads, the clank and hiss of machinery, and the sea frothing black coal dust on to the shore, she found it was the excitement that triumphed.

She would see her father! They managed once every three weeks, sometimes only once a month because of his shifts, but she would be with him for a couple of hours and talk to him, and maybe she could get him to tell her a little more about her mother; a little would do, she could live on a little. Then her brother might be in the house – and the four girls, two of them her stepsisters, the younger two her half-sisters. And Martha her stepmother. If only there were no Martha.

A child is helpless against the taunts of a fierce adult, and for as long as she could remember, Martha had 'got at her'. Her father intervened and sent Grace a sympathetic eye message from time to time but mostly he stayed out of it. 'Anything for a quiet life' was his excuse, his way of surviving. The work down the mines was hard. They ran under the sea and just to get to the coal face meant a back-bent walk of more than a mile. He was a willing provider and would always volunteer for extra shifts. He had never caught the habit of long stretches of quiet sleep. But at least Grace would see him, and the girls. She had bought sweets for them.

The town keyed up her exhilaration. It was barely believable that this coal and steel and steam town and her horse-powered village were on the same earth, let alone a few miles apart in the same county. The drama of the town seemed to prickle her skin into a full life-alert she felt rarely. So many men going to their work with such concentration; so many coal-smeared men returning from it with relief in their step, in the ease of tired shoulders. And the women, strong too, Grace thought, about their business.

Martha opened the door of the terraced house. 'I've told

you not to knock,' she said. 'Family and friends don't knock, they just walk in.'

She turned and Grace followed her, already sensing the rise of the dread. But when the girls waved and called her name across the small room, she was glad to be there. Only her father's daughters were there: Martha's own girls were out in the world, both married now.

'They'll be looking for their treats,' said Martha.

'Hello, lass.' Her father beckoned her to come to his chair by the fire. She bent down and he kissed her. Martha saw them twinned. Both had thick black hair, the strong blue eyes of the Irish who had come across to this west coast for work. Martha felt again a return of that anger at this girl who looked so like James's first wife – so he told her too often – and came here and queened it with her treats and her always clean clothes and her singing to the girls at the slightest opportunity.

'You'll want some tea?'

'I'll make it.'

'*I'll* make it. And they can have one sweet each and keep the rest for another time. We're not made of money in this house.'

James found Grace's eyes and soothed her. Just go with it, his look counselled her. Hold to what matters. And Grace always knew he had determinedly followed that through. James had sworn away his Roman Catholic faith, and he and her mother, Ruth, had married in the chapel at Oulton. They said it was a miserable affair. His Roman Catholic family did not come. Many of the Primitive Methodists did not want to be there. But Wilson said he knew a good man when he saw one and his was the final word. He warranted the marriage.

So James had learned to chain his anger and kept the

peace in his second home and tried to understand the anger of his second wife, who behaved like this only on the days when Grace visited them.

'Can I take the girls out for a walk?' Grace asked Martha.

'As long as you bring them back.'

'Why . . . I . . . I will.'

'Martha,' said James. And again. 'Martha.' Soothing her as he soothed Grace. 'Let her be.'

Martha turned her face away from him. 'You always take her side.'

'That's not true. And you know it's not true. But let them go out. Here. I'll stroll along a bit with them.'

'So it's a family outing. Am I not invited?'

'Yes. Come. Let's all go.'

'I've work to do,' said Martha. 'Somebody's got to get them their tea ready.'

'I could help,' said Grace, hopelessly.

'I don't need help. You just go and enjoy yourselves.'

On the street, Grace's heart soared when her father took her arm. 'You're a young woman now,' he said. 'They'll think I've clicked.'

The children scuttled around them and they walked down to the harbour. James nipped into a bakery and bought a loaf of old bread and split it into two parts, one each for the girls. They pinched pieces off it and threw it up for the seagulls to catch in mid-air or pick up off the sea. The fishermen were cleaning out their boats. The harbour was crowded with the Friday fleet. Grace felt that she was at a carnival.

An hour or so went by. The screaming calls of the gulls, the pride of the children filled with energy in the presence of their big sister.

James had the gift of easy talk and soon Grace felt she had

been with him for hours on end. Had her mother felt like this with him? A woman in the village had once told Grace that Ruth and James 'couldn't take their eyes off one another. In one way you couldn't have two people more different – Ruth on the farm, James the rolling stone who gathered no moss. And the religion, of course. But he turned up one haymaking when hands were needed and it seemed in no time at all they were talking wedding bells. Oh! What a commotion that was! A Roman Catholic!' she said. 'It was a revolution round here – but your mother wouldn't give in and neither would he. They were just made for each other. It was something to see.'

Grace carried that around with her like a locket. 'Made for each other'. She opened it only when she felt unaccountably lonely and breathed it in. Now, with her father, as the boats rolled gently on the water and the lights were lit against the darkness, she felt that she could understand it.

'Better go back,' said James.

They went back, the four of them, in what for Grace was like a dream, walking through the gloaming of the streets. The rows and rows of terraced houses were lit up now and it was a warm house that met them when they walked in.

Martha came across to James directly and stood toe to toe with him. 'What time do you call this?'

'We were feeding the gulls.'

'Well, you can feed yourselves now. It's wasted.'

'Martha. It'll be all right.'

'Not when she's around,' the older woman said spitefully. 'It always ends like this when she comes – we always have an argument.'

'I'm not arguing.'

'I'll go now,' said Grace. 'There's a train soon.'

'I'll set you to the station,' he said.

'You've just come back with her!'

'I'll be back before you know it.'

'Well, you might not find me here.'

The children were cowed but Grace was not going to go without giving them a kiss. From Martha's expression it was as if she were planting a stigma on their faces.

'She's been badly,' said James, as they stood on the platform. 'Her nerves seem to have gone. She can't help herself. I think she's got something and she's scared. She should go to the doctor but she won't. She wasn't herself, Grace.'

Grace nodded, unwilling to waste a minute on her, unable to forgive. The train pulled in. James opened the carriage door for her and gave a little bow. 'My turn to come over to see you, next time,' he said. 'You'll see that I will.'

She waited until the train was well clear of the town and then, in the empty carriage, the girl wept her heart out and felt the terrible pain of a jealousy she did not understand.

CHAPTER EIGHT

The next morning, after chapel, Grace, as usual took Belle around to their mother's grave. It was a cold morning, a north wind whipping across the plain, and Belle, who felt the cold, decided to stay for no more than a few moments. Grace was relieved when she left. To want to be alone was selfish, she knew that, but her yearning for solitude was sometimes strong and occasionally, as on this Sunday morning, desperate.

She looked at the neatly trimmed mound and the plain granite headstone and tried to summon up thoughts that would do justice to the turbulence of her feelings. In the novels she read thoughts seemed so well ordered. In her mind there was a constellation of perplexities that would not settle down into anything resembling the coherent sentences in the books she liked so much. So she stood, quite still, letting the wind blow about her, a lone figure in the small graveyard. Mr Walker saw her as he left the chapel: the minister hesitated and then he sensed that such spellbound stillness wanted no interruption and went his Sabbath way.

Sunday was the Lord's Day and his day too, and Mr Walker felt it keenly as he strolled around the village pacing out the boundaries of his parish. He loved the difference of the Sabbath. Every shop was closed. When people emerged from their homes they would be dressed at least respectably and most often in their solely once-a-week-worn black Sunday Best. There was neither sowing nor ploughing on a Sunday, neither harvest nor haymaking. Now and then a pony trap would take people to visit relatives or a family walking party would go down the lane past the village hall to the little tarn beyond which the gypsies used to camp in the winter. With a west wind you could sometimes hear the bells from the churches in Wigton. The Bible would still be read in some of the cottages he walked past. It was called the day of rest. Only a few failed to mark it. Across most of the land it was a day when another way of the world was observed and villages, towns, hamlets and cities were linked to keep it as they thought it had been immemorially observed.

Grace had walked from the grave to her favourite view-point on a small rise of land from which she could look down to the Solway Firth and across to Scotland and, in the right light, catch the sheen from the sliver of sea. She wanted to break out of this Sunday and all Sundays. Her agitation had become a mind and body torment through a restless night. She wanted to race, to hurl herself into some great adventure, to leap off this little mound of earth and soar over the plain, over the sea. She remembered the ballad 'Over the Sea to Skye'.

How could she miss so achingly someone she had never known? How could that happen? Her mother was in her grave, nearly fourteen years dead now, never seen, never heard and yet staked inside Grace. She felt tears inside her and flushed at the thought that somebody might have come into that compartment of the train and seen her in tears the previous evening. Grace never cried, they said, but there she had been weeping, and in a public place.

She tried to understand. In his sermon Mr Walker had

spoken about how you could change yourself and how you must change yourself. He had spoken of the rich man who had given up all his wealth and the poor men who had given up their work as fishermen and Saul who had given up his life at Damascus to become St Paul; Grace was near blushing. She had thought this was somehow directed at her. How could she be so vain? And yet it had seemed so clearly meant for her. In little more than a week the pupil-teacher proposition had seeped into the whisperings of the village and Grace felt cut off by it. She sensed envy. She sensed an unusual tension between her grandmother and her grandfather. She had become a little distant from Miss Errington.

She wanted to fly away and yet, looking down on the ample lap of the plain land, the first mountains of Scotland beyond, the last of England behind, she felt a security stemming from the earth itself. Here she was planted. So where did it come from, this opposite power, this almost panic, to get away, to uproot herself?

Only when she felt thoroughly cold did she wrench herself away and hurry back home.

~

Grace was in the front schoolroom when it happened. Miss Errington was clearing up the senior room at the back.

The shouting had been nothing out of the ordinary but a shriller element and then the unmistakable voice of Belle sent Grace to the window and from there, blind with anger, gorged with it from that first sight, to the school gate.

Three of them were baiting, tormenting Belle: one boy, Daniel Turnbull, a swarthy man of a boy, son of one of the grander farmers, and the two sisters who came from that clump of poor cottages near the tarn settlement, forever desolate and home of toxic rumours. They circled Belle like wolves around a deer, they dashed forward to prod her or slap her or tug at her hair. The girls spat at her; the swarthy boy made a jeering farting sound and put his thumbs to his ears and wriggled his fingers and gaped a smile of pleasure as Belle's distress became more and more visible. As Grace flew across the playground she saw the feeble flailing of Belle's unwilling arms. And as she came nearer, she caught full sight of the terror in her sister's eyes. 'Leave off my sister! Leave off my sister!'

Grace grabbed the hair of both girls and pulled them to the ground and attempted to drag them away. The boy came near and she hit out at him and screamed at him and when he stood struck dumb, she let the girls go for a moment and leaped at him to scratch his face, claw down it, draw blood, and when he kicked out she caught the lumpen boot and yanked it high so that he fell back and smacked his head on the ground. The two sisters had got up and stood side by side, warily. This time Grace whirled her arms and ran at them, all the time shouting abuse at them, swearing and howling, and did not mind the blows she received and would not have cared if they had felled her to the ground as long as she could hurt these people, as long as she could harm them and take revenge for her sister, who had now stood aside, making a strange noise as she sobbed and tried not to sob. The two girls got Grace on the ground and were kicking her, and Daniel stood above her, waiting to join in.

It was at this stage that Miss Errington appeared.

'Grace was like a banshee,' she said to Wilson and Sarah. They had been shocked at the state of Belle and Grace when they came home, but unable to get anything out of either of them. Miss Errington, to her credit, they thought, had come to the house to explain everything even though it was well into the evening. She, too, was distressed.

'I could not believe it of her,' she said. 'She was like a wild creature.'

'There must have been a reason,' said Wilson.

'Nothing could excuse that.'

'We should know the reason,' he said.

'It seems that the Turnbull boy and the McQuinn girls were teasing Belle.' She paused. 'And hitting her.'

'The McQuinns can be difficult,' said Sarah, 'but Belle often turns up to meet Grace after school. What happened today?'

'I don't know,' said Miss Errington, although she had her suspicions.

The favouring of Grace had not gone down well with all the pupils. Talk of Grace's possible further education might have stirred the pot. Belle, as a defenceless one, had through the years been well protected at school, first of all by Miss Errington herself and then by Grace. But Miss Errington knew that there were devils out there in the world. She had seen gargoyles on churches to fight off the devils that tried to destroy those churches and she had understood them. She had seen boys and some girls do unforgivable things to each other. And at times there would be a spiralling down, a devil's whirlpool, an unleashing of nastiness that sucked out all goodness and reason and would not be satisfied until it spent the dark force that drove it. Miss Errington had seen that a few times in her teaching life and it frightened her. It came out of a part of humanity she did not want to acknowledge. It sought only to torture and destroy and once it had identified a victim, there was joy as well as energy in the hunt to kill.

'Belle and Grace are very upset,' said Sarah. 'They're in their room.'

'We must clear it up,' said the schoolteacher. 'I've been to see the other two families and the children will apologise to Belle tomorrow. I will make them do that after morning prayers in front of the whole school. The parents agree. In fact Mr McQuinn started to slap his daughters in front of me and I had to ask him to stop.' She paused. 'And I think it would be good if Grace were to apologise too.'

Wilson held his tongue.

Sarah said, 'Should I bring them down?'

While she went to fetch them, Wilson added coal to the fire but maintained his silence.

The girls edged into the room and Miss Errington was shocked by the change that had come over Grace. Something ... violent about her, still. Belle sat down and lowered her head as if awaiting a sentence. Grace, beside her, looked at Miss Errington full in the face.

It was explained that the others had agreed to apologise to Belle. Belle was asked if she would come to the school in the morning and, after looking to Sarah, to Wilson and to Grace, she nodded. Grace held out her hand to her sister, who clasped it desperately.

'And,' said Miss Errington, 'I think that if you were to say you were sorry, Grace, then we could put all this behind us.'

'Who to? Who do I say I'm sorry to?'

'Those you attacked.'

'They were getting Belle.'

'Your behaviour was too violent, Grace. It was far more violent than it need have been.'

'I won't apologise. I'm not sorry.'

'When you think about it, overnight, I believe you will find it the better way. To turn the other cheek. To forgive your enemies. To bless them that curse you.'

Grace did not respond.

Is this the same girl? Miss Errington wondered. Is this the girl I have seen grow so finely 'through sun and shower'? How can people change so? Yet look at the others, Turnbull and the McQuinns. They were generally obedient enough, uninterested but not disruptive, nothing that could not be quelled. And then this wickedness.

She worried about Wilson. There had been a difference in him during the discussion. It was as if he had absented himself from the person Miss Errington had known before this incident and left only a trace of himself in the room. She felt tired and rather dizzy.

'It would mean a lot to all of us, Grace,' the schoolteacher said, with difficulty, meaning 'It would mean a lot to me', 'if you did feel you could apologise. Say that you were sorry you had ... behaved ... like that ... like ...' To her horror she almost said 'an animal'. 'Not like you, Grace.'

But Grace stayed silent. The girl felt that she had gone into a deep vault and locked herself in there where no one could enter and she would not hear what anyone said. She was very hungry. Belle's head had sunk even lower as the tension inside her sister streamed into her, as Grace's strong feelings always did.

'We'll have to let her sleep on it,' said Wilson. 'She'll be at the school in the morning.'

Refusing the cup of tea she desperately wanted, Miss Errington took her leave, pausing in front of Grace for a sign, getting nothing save for a politely chiselled 'Goodnight, Miss.'

Even though Mr Walker got involved, Grace would not apologise and Wilson, who alone might have forced her into it, would not intervene.

Her refusal became her fate. The enthusiasm and affection that had gone into the pupil-teacher notion drained

73

away. There were those who admired Grace for what she had done; a few who saw her as a cross between a local heroine and a martyr, but they did not hold sway. Her school days ended with the prize for best pupil, a special mention from Miss Errington in her round-up of the year, but they ended. Her formal education was done and she was now out in the world.

CHAPTER NINE

'Where've you been?'

'I was here yesterday.'

'You weren't.'

'I was. You won't remember.'

'My memory's terrible sometimes. It's just terrible.'

She put her hands to her head. Her expression was normal and unclouded. It was the lapses into normality that made John most sorry for her. Did she look around, in those moments, and see the wreckage and know it for what it was? Did this brief emergence show her what had been and could never be again? The pain of that. It was not just that her memory returned although it was a bit stronger. It was that she spoke coherently, held a conversation for a while, cut her way through the spreading tendrils of destruction that were strangling the cells of memory, feeding on her past and leaving her starved of it. Did she have a clear intimation of this? If so, how could she bear it? How could anyone bear it?

'I won't get better, will I?'

'Well . . . there are some days you . . .'

'I won't get better.' She looked away from him and then said, emphatically, 'They should put us down.'

He was winded. So matter-of-fact. So meant.

'Come on, then, what are we going to talk about?' she said briskly. 'None of them talk round here. They just sit.'

'The nurses talk.'

'They do. I'll give them that. You talk now.'

'When you married Dad you had to leave the factory, Redmayne's, didn't you?'

'We all had to. All the women had to leave when they got married.'

'Did you like the factory?'

'I liked the women. We'd all been at school together. I liked being with them. You had to wait to get a job there. It took me six months. But I didn't like our boss. He would walk up and down between the machines like a slave driver. 'Hurry up now, girls!' 'Don't do this.' 'Why are you doing that?' None of us liked him. But you couldn't say anything. We would sing in the dinner break and he didn't like that but we got up a deputation to Mr Redmayne himself and he was a gentleman and he said, 'Let the girls sing. It will exercise their lungs!' Mary laughed, a clear, untroubled laugh, and John felt an ice-melt of recognition. '"It will exercise their lungs!"' she repeated happily.

He so rarely could ask her questions beyond 'How are you?' or 'Do you feel well today?' A desert. This was a sudden oasis. It was like it had been, times past. He could ask her about herself. And yet he had never wanted to or perhaps never dared to ask her personal questions. Or any, come to think. There was that about her private personality which was irrevealable. Anything that threatened to draw her into a confidential expression or an explanation of herself was not to be raised. She was easy and casual with issues and the events of the day; she liked the gossip of the town, which was her fiction; but now, about to open an innocent line of enquiry, John felt that he must tread very carefully.

She was still alert: eager, upright in the bed, her white nightgown like a surplice around her neck, her hair just 'done' that morning, a helmet of silver white.

'Well, then?'

He risked it. 'When you left the factory, why did you choose to have fish knives?'

'You were offered a set of fish knives or a prodded rug,' she said. 'That was what you got for going.'

'Why didn't you choose the prodded rug?'

She might have sensed or invented that John was being critical of her rejection of that undoubtedly more common item. Prodded rugs were mats or, pushing it, carpets of varying sizes. They were made from remnants of any old scraps of material, which were prodded, with a bodkin, through a hessian base. Few ordinary homes were without them. Most people made their own, the rug hanging behind the door, reminding any visitors they could bring a few scraps and prod them in with the bodkin. There were women who were very talented at this craft and they could produce patterned rugs and even figurative rugs – a cockerel, an eagle – rugs you would be proud to keep. Redmayne's would order one of these for the young female who was to be fired for matrimony. Mary took John's enquiry to be a criticism: that somehow, by not choosing a prodded rug, she was committing the sin of 'getting above herself'.

'I like a prodded rug,' she said.

'I know.'

'There's nothing wrong with a prodded rug.'

'I know. I know.'

'*Everybody* likes them.'

'They do. I do. Everybody does.'

Usually he would have backed off. But today he was

encouraged by the coherence of her attention. 'But you chose the fish knives and forks.'

'I did,' she said, after a few moments, which might have been reflection.

John remembered those knives and forks. He had first come across them when he was four or five. They were tucked away at the bottom of a bed-linen chest he was excavating at the time. He pulled out the green case as if he had stumbled into Ali Baba's cave.

The cheap imitation green leather, pocked like crocodile skin, was clearly, to him, a casket fit to hold treasure. He found the little gold-looking hooks and snapped them open and there they were, displayed before him. Six forks, very thin but exotic, and six things that looked like knives but had no real blade and were very easy to bend. Silver, he was sure of that. Each one was secured in two slots in the casket, head and tail, and the set of twelve rested on a soft purple material. His mother told him that they were fish knives and that they were special.

From then on and as the years passed by he kept encountering them. Once when he was about thirteen and off school with some infectious complaint, he tried to kill the boredom by opening every drawer in his parents' bedroom, trying on clothes, puzzled by some of his discoveries, aroused to a rather agreeable state of guilty excitement, and he came across them again. This time they were with the gloves and scarves. And again he looked in and again they intrigued him and still they had never been used.

Later in his adolescent reading he found that the poet John Betjeman thought that fish knives were common. That puzzled him. They were, he thought, unmistakably grand. Later he learned that Betjeman's aped upper-class snobbery was contradicted by the real aristocrats, whose dinner tables had long been furnished with fish knives. He felt his mother had been vindicated. He was ridiculously pleased that his mother's taste was upheld at that high court.

The last time he had seen them was when he was in the bathroom looking for a razor blade in the old chest of drawers to which everything that might come in useful in the future was condemned. Once more he opened the green box, which was by now to him something of a sacred object. The knives and forks had fallen on hard times. The damp of the bathroom had rusted them, the velvet was faded, the little snip catches were broken. They were of no further use.

They had never once been put on the table.

The only fish he could remember them eating in his childhood had come from the fish-and-chip shop and was so coated in an armour of batter that the puny forks would have buckled in any attempt to break through to the cod.

'Why did you choose the fish knives?'

She did not like the interrogation but there was still some energy left. 'I like fish,' she said.

'But we never used them for fish. And if we had used them for the fish from Josie's . . . Josie's fish needed proper knives.'

'You never know,' she said, 'we might have had guests.'

John knew he should have left it at that. He could not remember any guests who had ever come to eat. 'Guests' was too grand a word. People dropped in for a cup of tea and maybe a biscuit. 'Guests' was a blind. Both of them knew it. He was sitting at the end of the bed. She had lowered her head, all but hiding her face. A lock of her hair swung down across her brow and when, defiantly, she looked up at him, her slim face, he would have sworn, had a look, sweet, mischievous, that took it back to the day she had been presented with that set of fish knives.

'So why,' he asked, and it would be for the last time, 'did you choose the fish knives?'

Suddenly, she smiled, and swung her head, with a gesture that was both old and young, and said, 'Swank! Just swank!'

He clapped his hands, he wanted to cheer: she was back! And there was more. Surfing on the wave, she held out her left arm and began to sing. Her actions followed the words of the simple song they would all sing together at the socials, the whole room, all ages, in a circle, like a primitive ritual chant.

> 'You put your left arm in,
> Your left arm out,
> In out, in out,
> You shake it all about.'

She shook her arm vigorously. John joined in.

> 'You do the hokey-cokey
> And you turn around.'

She swayed from side to side in her bed.

> 'That's what it's all about.'

Their voices rose and the nurse who had stopped outside beckoned a fellow nurse and her patient in a wheelchair to listen.

> 'Oh! Hokey-cokey-cokey.
> Oh! Hokey-cokey-cokey.
> Oh! Hokey-cokey-cokey.
> Knees bent, arms stretch

Arm in, arm out,
Rah! rah! rah!'

The eavesdropping audience in the corridor took up the song.

'You put your right arm in,
Your right arm out,
In out, in out,
You shake it all about.
You do the hokey-cokey
And you turn around.
That's what it's all about.'

The audience and the chorus swelled along the corridors of the nursing home as they all sang.

'Oh! Hokey-cokey-cokey.
Oh! Hokey-cokey-cokey.
Oh! Hokey-cokey-cokey.
Knees bent, arms stretch
Arm in, arm out,
Rah! rah! rah!'

'I don't think we can do the legs bit,' said Mary, looking down at the blankets that covered them.

'That was fine,' he said. That was wonderful! he thought. That was the best time we have had for weeks! he thought. And fish knives and 'Swank!' But she did not like compliments. So, 'Fine,' he repeated, and let it go.

Outside, the audience dispersed, taking a cheerful singing mood to the next destination.

John went on to the beach for an hour to let the pleasure

settle, to bask in it; even to hope. The flat dullness of the day only made more vivid the almost absurd intoxication he felt. What if, in time for her, the research on Alzheimer's could make sufficient progress? If she could snap back like that for about twenty minutes, perhaps in some ways she could be again as she had been. Could they not freeze-photograph her mind in those minutes and find a way to re-create it, to use that lucidity as a basis?

He lit a cigarette and walked swiftly over the wet flat sands, loving the whip of wind on his face, the chill and bite of it. It was 'only' an illness, after all. Other illnesses, diseases, plagues had been cured. Every year new science brought new cures. Why not for this? He would go on to the Internet again when he got back to London in a few hours.

But to be alive, he thought, as he strode beside the incoming sea and looked at the cargoes of heavy cloud, just to breathe in the air, to look at and recognise what you saw, to know that you were here, now, and to have the good fortune to enjoy it. Just to be. That was what he wanted for her. To be and to know it.

The journey south would take about five hours, depending on the traffic. He loaded up a CD selection and drove back into the metropolis with its rolling crises, back to the drip, drip, drip of unanswerable questions and his own ageing problems of health murmurs and pensions and downsizing and what future for his children. Yet for John the city was still intoxicating. When it finally swallowed him and he was on automatic in the last streets, he raked over the best things of the day, and laughed out loud, as the headlights sliced through the over-lit streets.

Oh! Hokey-cokey-cokey.
Oh! Hokey-cokey-cokey.

Oh! Hokey-cokey-cokey.
In out, in out,
Rah! rah! rah!

'Just swank!' he said aloud. 'Just swank.' And he loved her for it.

He turned into his London street after midnight, a few lights, shine on the road from recent rain, a sudden exhaustion.

CHAPTER TEN

They kept her on the farm. It was not a decision taken with the long term in mind, it just fell out that way. All of them were shaken by the incident at the school gates. Wilson gave little sign but Grace was aware of a hesitation over her now, so slight, so very slight, but she knew him well. Sarah's reaction was to be more energetic in her dealings with her granddaughter, and rather more encouraging than before. Belle, for weeks, trod in her sister's footsteps and feared to let her out of her sight.

Grace felt that she was no longer her old self but what she had become she did not know. 'Out of sorts' was the phrase that Sarah used to Wilson when they talked about her. He would not demur but in a way that he could not articulate he thought the incident showed that there was something deeply worrying in her. She would find life very difficult, he thought. She had snapped and there was now seen to be a flaw in her character.

The pupil-teacher dream had pushed aside the need for planning what she should do on finishing school. Now, when asked, she was not helpful or even sensible. It seemed to Wilson that she was determined to annoy him. Her answers had included 'Run away to sea' and 'Work in the flour mills in Silloth with the other girls'. She had to be reined in, he thought; and perhaps that included the notion that she had to be broken in. So they kept her on the farm, kept her under surveillance.

Mr Walker had failed to save Grace and he found it hard to forgive himself. He had a partiality for her, viewed closely and rather jealously by Miss Errington.

He had let it settle and then the minister had gone to the school to make a last plea to Miss Errington. He spoke of forgiveness and cited Christ's tolerance of sinners and pointed out the power of repentance. But Miss Errington would not be moved. It was not so much the violence as the lack of that repentance he spoke about. She feared that Grace had a devil in her and, although she put this very tentatively, she was surprised that the minister had not noticed it. The pupil-teacher arrangement would be far too great a risk. Miss Errington was obdurate.

He left the schoolroom and made his way to the river. Sometimes he feared for the future of his religion. It was too harsh, he thought. What would not bend would surely break. He saw all around him the lush, yielding fertility of the plain and he felt a fear that the stoniness of the path he preached did not reflect the rich and varied world of God. But his mission was to serve and he prayed aloud and returned home more resolute.

The months, from summer when she left school until the closing down of late autumn, from the hay turning and harvest to potato picking, were always the busiest span. She was scarcely in the house and the long days both tested and tired her. She worked alongside the hired men, and now that she was hour by hour with them, they let her harness and lead the horses. They were impressed as the sheaves of hay she swung on to the cart grew in volume over the haymaking time and soon little competitions grew between them.

There was a cheerfulness on the farm that Wilson had not known before and the effect Grace had on everyone eased his anxiety.

She was a young woman now. Sarah was on the lookout for the beginning of Grace's periods and helped her cope with the onset. When 'the time of the month' arrived, Grace was soon able to steer herself through it. Through these and other physical confidences, Sarah's trust began to be restored.

She wanted to make Grace feel needed. She decided that she would not wait for the spring to do her annual 'clean through', but give the house a once-in-a-lifetime scouring, painting, papering. Grace would be the perfect helper and Belle would be led to feel useful. Wilson, not at all keen, surrendered after Sarah's glinting comment that 'Best get it all sorted out while we can.' He yielded. But as a man embedded in the farmhouse, and well satisfied to see every article where it had always been, he braced himself.

So that Grace and Belle would not think of themselves any longer as schoolgirls, Wilson decided to give them a wage. He sat both of them down and told them what it would cost for him to hire women to do the work they were doing. He then deducted their 'keep', including clothes, and kept back a percentage that he would save for them, and when it reached a steady sum he would add it to their bank accounts, opened some years before and increased each year by the proceeds from the sale of their lambs. The modest sum that remained for their pocket was more or less the same as the other working girls and young women in the village received. Did they think it was fair? he asked. They agreed that it was and left the room a little gravely, feeling that they had experienced their first significant adult meeting. Belle said she would give her money to Grace to keep for her. She would tie it up in a handkerchief, she said, so that Grace would know which was hers.

Grace was to stay on the farm for the next three years. The incident at the school gates drifted into the byways of memory. There was a village choir and Grace never missed a practice. It was a time of competitions and the choir went to Wigton and Silloth and further afield to the industrial coast, to Whitehaven and Workington where the mining families prided themselves on their music. One year they got into the finals at the big festival in the market hall in the county town: Carlisle.

For Grace singing in the choir was almost a form of self-hypnosis, a forgetting of herself, another life. It was like lying deep in that goosefeather mattress with the merest sough of wind in the sycamores beyond the garden, the slightest rattle of the window panes, just a reminder there was a real world out there. The goosefeather mattress could wrap round her like a cocoon and so could the choir, other voices, her own scarcely heard but part of this flow, part of the sea of sound on which she seemed to float.

There were village dances now and then to raise money for the chapel or the school or the Friendly Society or the old people's fund. Oulton had its own small carnival every summer with the floats on the back of the carts and the silver band brought in from Wigton. There were outings and trips to Port Carlisle to swim in the sea, and in the warm evenings they would play rounders sometimes with the boys. Sundays took care of themselves. There was time for walks and time for reading. She went to Wigton to a newsagent once a fortnight on Friday evenings. For a small charge, she borrowed two books, always novels, which she would more devour than read and, if they captured her, she would close the book only to pause for the aftertaste of it and then open to start it again.

On those Fridays she would buy a newspaper, choosing the one with the most photographs.

There she saw the Great World. She saw the aristocracy in full plumage, shiny top hats and smart uniforms for the men, coats and gowns that trailed to the floor, scintillating tiaras and a lushness of jewellery for the women, fine horses, homes like palaces, and she dreamed alongside them. She read of strikes in the London docks and learned of the grievances of angry men and found that she could sympathise with them too. She read of theatres and balls, of Ascot and Henley. There were reports of the doings in Parliament and accounts of events in other countries in the empire, which made her relieved to be English but also jealous of the dramas other people had. The novels brought the world of imagination, the newspapers an equally foreign picture of the world she lived in so marginally. She saw herself as one who only peeped into the country to which she belonged. It passed her by. It was the novels that most often spoke to her condition and circumstances.

These years, before the outbreak of the First World War, were often remembered as a sweet and unrecapturable time of balm, a perpetual summer of content, an apotheosis of the best of country and empire with all the darkness and injustice and cruelty later erased from the picture. It began a romance. It was seen as a time of the gentle greatness of this sceptred island. Lost for ever, it merged into myth. And Grace, too, was to remember it as a haze of happiness and friendliness. It was her youth that was happy and her character that was friendly but the world seemed to reflect her. And there were the scents of love.

She had in her the spoor of her sex without recognising it, hardly acknowledging it, but it was there. As she picked up the looks and the suggestions of two or three of the young men, she felt herself react and began to know that she was desired and that she, too, could desire.

The thicketed winding lane to the tarn and the banks of the slender willow-strewn streams trickling slowly towards the sea became the sets for courting. Boys who at school had been clumsy, snotty-nosed and grubby were now taller, larky and rather attractive in their long trousers and jaunty caps. They made a ritual of it. The girls, three or four of them, would walk down the lane and meet the boys walking up the lane. The boys would pause for a few inarticulate minutes, walk on and then turn back down the lane to meet the girls walking up the lane. That lane became erotic. A conversation would develop, often shy, lumpen, agricultural and expressed in embarrassed fragments but sometimes a sentence would lead to a paragraph. As the weeks went on, they began to regain the easy chatter that had characterised their early childhood, and the purpose emerged.

Very gradually, they began to peel off in pairs. The pairings followed intense discussion in both camps. The boys resorted to a clumsy bashing of each other on the arms or even lightly wrestling with each other as they strove to direct their unbearable lusts into acceptable manoeuvres. There was much talk of who fancied whom and who might be fancied by whom and why this one was a turnip, that one a sleek little calf, the other a foxy thing. At times all the lads swore that none of the girls was worth the treasure of their attention. At times they realised that any girl would do as long as she rid him of this awful sexual ache.

The girls were scarcely more genteel, although they thought they were. They, too, could be savage in their comments. This one was as ugly as a wart, that one as dozy as an old ram, that one with a bit of the tinker about him. None of them was worth the trouble and certainly did not merit the charms and attention of such young women as themselves.

And so they would go to the walk along the banks of the stream only to find that the cluster of boys had taken exactly the same notion save that they were walking on the other side of the stream. For some reason the boys started to throw pebbles into the water, near the edge of the opposite bank where, with luck, they would raise a splash. And the girls, every one of whom had, most likely, that day been in farm-yard sluther and field mud, and carried muck-covered piles of wood, or dug-up vegetables, would shriek and scamper away like coy nymphs.

Until, it seemed, one evening, the gavotte was over and all of them had paired off, going their individual ways, finding their own private paths along the sheep tracks and over-grown bridleways, to begin the next stage, most often in profound silence.

At first Grace had her eye on Thomas Pennington. He was the best looker although, unfortunately, he knew it. But, still, there was no denying it. There was a cut about his clothes and his manner that reflected the high status of his family in the village. He tended to find ways to refer to aspects of that superiority, which could be rather embar-rassing but, still, what he boasted of was what he had. Grace was attracted to him even though she felt he rather took it for granted that she would be, that any girl would be, that there could well be a queue of girls from Oulton across the marshes to the sea all in a line waiting for Thomas Pennington to say yes. Nevertheless, despite all that, he was the big catch and she knew she had hooked him.

But it was soon clear to Grace, when they peeled off together and walked thigh deep in the tresses of barley, when they stopped for no reason other than to summon up the nerve for a kiss although somebody might be looking, that something was wrong. Grace did not know what was wrong but she knew it was there. He did not seem to feel, she thought. But then, quite soon, she came to the conclusion that feeling was not his strong suit. There was a sense in him that the job had been done and all that remained was to get on with it. She felt like an acquisition – a pleasant and useful one, and quite ornamental, but no more than a necessary addition to the estate of Thomas Pennington. One evening he told her that his mother had said she measured up quite well but needed a bit of reining in and the sooner he did it the better.

She chucked him.

It seemed for a while as if she had missed out. There was not a wide choice in the first place and the good ones and even the good-enough ones had paired up. Thomas was soon snapped up by Marjorie Paisley who had no qualms about chucking Alan King. Alan King was no good for Grace: there was, she told Belle, very little there in the thinking department. She walked alone, which had its own little frisson of pleasure, or with Belle, ever heavier and slower but of whom she never tired.

Frank came out of the blue. Grace thought he was like Baby Bear's porridge – just right. She set herself at Frank, and a wild Gay Gordons at the Christmas dance in the village hall settled the matter, and publicly.

Frank's father had a substantial farm down on the plain near the sea. There were two sisters and four brothers and for Frank, the youngest, there was not enough work. He had come to work with his uncle at Oulton. Eventually the ambition was that the home farm would be sufficiently extended by rent or purchase to employ all the brothers.

Grace felt very easy with him. He was tall, loosely built,

strong like all the lads but lithe too. He liked horse-riding and exercised the two hunters of Miss Birkett who lived in Oulton Manor. Grace would spot him some early mornings, his flaxen-haired head above the hedge-tops, riding one, leading one, his back straight. Soon they were together. If he took only one of the horses out of an evening, he would turn down a rarely trodden track and meet her and hoist her up behind him and she would clutch him round the waist, the warm body of the horse exciting both of them, and he would look for a stretch of open ground to break into a gallop. Even then he was steady.

Usually their encounters were more sober. A walk, most of all, walking was the thing – or, rather, strolling. There was no concept of exercise: their days were laden with physical labour. Walking was for companionability or a meditative interval in a life of constant and heavy work.

They were, the village said, 'a good-looking couple'. Grace, dark, quick; Frank more ambling, blond, freckled, with the aspect of someone who had all the time in the world. Grace appeared to glide or skid over the surface, depending on her mood. Frank seemed hewn out of centuries of agriculture down on the plain next to the marshland and the sea. On the plain the seasons moved through without harm and they had always benefited from them or outwitted them. The soil, they said, was as rich as any in England. The sea brought a tang to the air – the fishermen were good company and good for barter. On the marshes the labourers dug up the peat and fires could burn cheaply the year round. Frank was unshakeable and Grace felt a powerful sense of relief, which she decided was love.

He was amused that she read books she did not have to read. His book days had begun and ended in school. Now he read a few pages of the local newspaper every Friday

– concentrating on the market prices for cattle, sheep and pigs and dwelling on any story that was gruesome. She told him he was illiterate, which made him smile and nod in agreement. She could read for both of them, he said.

Sometimes she tried to tease him into a temper. She would be deliberately late just to test him. He would be sitting on the hedge bank, whittling away at a piece of wood or smoking, calm as a pond, and no mention of her lack of punctuality. She would criticise the limited lives and low horizons of the local community and in her criticism become quite cutting about their lack of vim and 'go'. They were sticks-in-the-mud. Sleepwalkers. Trudging over the land like dumb animals more than people full of life. Farmers were especially hopeless – content to do the same old things year in and year out until Doomsday.

Frank said that could very well be true, it wouldn't surprise him. So what was he going to do about it? He would give her a kiss. He was unteasable and she did not want to hurt his feelings by provoking his jealousy, which, happily, she knew was there. Soon she gave up her feeble campaign and decided that he was the 'answer to a maiden's prayer'. That made him laugh, when she told him. He thought it was 'about right!' and that easy unboast made her feel tender to him.

A maiden she was. There was eagerness and lust in both of them but there was compelling restraint. After a few months, they had marriage in view but both of them accepted that it was some years down the line. They had to save, they had to be capable of independence; above all, they had to wait to get older. There would be no risks taken and in the near background for both of them were the strictures of their chapels. But they found ways, and delay and antici-pation had their own sexual satisfactions.

One fine autumn evening, when she had been with

Frank and ridden the second horse as she had begun to do in the evenings, she came back later than usual and knew as she opened the farm gate that something was wrong, that something terrible, awful, had happened. And she knew it was Belle.

Belle had been in the orchard helping to pick the apples. They had let her go up the ladder to reach the highest ones. Grace used to do that job. She would never allow her sister to do it, however much she pleaded. Taking advantage of Grace's absence, Belle had wheedled to get her own way and climbed clumsily, heaving her heavy body slowly but excitingly to the very top of the long wooden ladder. There she had reached out and plucked the rose-faced fruits and popped them into the deep pocket on the front of her pinny.

High above the trees, the village, the world of her life, was in view for her as never before, the sun to the west across the sea, shooting sheets of crimson through the low-lying clouds. Belle swayed forward and back in delight. If only Grace could see her, and the store in her pouch grew and she felt the heaviness of it, the achievement of it, and swayed back to seize the scene around her, to take every bit of joy from the miraculous moment. And fell down to the hard ground.

'She would have felt nothing,' Sarah repeated, like a constant prayer. 'Dr Nicholson said that she would have felt nothing at all.'

Grace said, more than once, 'I should have been there.' And at night in their bed she keened 'like a trapped animal', Wilson said.

The village closed down for the funeral.

CHAPTER ELEVEN

He took in two books of old photographs, which he hoped would catch her attention. One contained about fifty photographs of Wigton in the first half of the twentieth century, the other a bigger area including the town but spread out across the Solway Plain. The photographs were all in black and white, mostly taken by local enthusiasts. There were short explanatory paragraphs attached to each of them.

John sat on the bed alongside her and began with the book on Old Wigton. First he riffled through it to show how much there was and how it was worth a span of attention. Often when he brought her a magazine or a newspaper she would study the first page and then go no further. This time he needed to be cunning. He thought she would love it.

He had not anticipated how much she would love it.

'Where did you get this?'

'In Winters. In the shop on the corner.'

'How can anybody afford to buy this?'

'It was very reasonable.'

'It must be worth a fortune. A fortune! It must be! Just look at all those wonderful photographs!' She put the book on the bed for a moment, overcome. She was weak with the impact of her past: the joy of it, the presence of it, its unexpected entrances into her lonely afternoon.

He said nothing for some moments as she kept glancing at the cover of the book. It was a detailed view of the high street in Wigton on a market day at the beginning of the twentieth century. A single, stately, broad-beamed, open-topped motor-car going down the street of cobbled stones and horse droppings brought to an entranced standstill the market crowd. There were horses and carts, flocks of people around the open-air stalls, awnings shading some of the shops, shops she would have used – Aird's the ironmonger, John Studholme the boot-, shoe- and clog-maker. There was the Fountain House Inn, and above its door a coloured glass barrel with gas lamps to drum up trade in the evenings. There were dogs and children, men in sober suits, all booted and hatted, women in long dresses and mostly hatted. The street itself had not changed much to the present day.

'You would think they were alive,' she said. 'You just have to wave a wand and they'll all start walking and talking.'

She made the photograph alive for John as much as for herself. For most others it was a charming record, part of a local pictorial chronicle, one of hundreds like it all over the country in the thriving grip of nostalgia. For Mary, bringing to it her beholder's share, her place in it, it was not just a history but an autobiography, an anthology evoking sounds and smells as well as sights, of neighbours and friends, of articles bought in those shops and vegetables purchased from the country women who came into the town on the medieval-chartered Tuesday market day. It was a picture from her life and she brimmed with it, too full of it to say anything for a while, too occupied in receiving and sifting the impressions and the detail of an existence from this one black-and-white photograph.

He picked up the book and turned over the pages slowly, sometimes pausing to read the descriptive paragraphs, sometimes not needing to as she supplied her own. 'That's the station,' she said. 'That was at the bottom of our street.' 'That's the Methodist church,' said John. 'Studholmes!' she said. 'Look at them! One, two, three, four, five, six men and a boy. In that little shoe shop. Six men and a boy.' 'It says that shoes and boots were hand-repaired there and clogs were made. You wore clogs, didn't you?' 'Everybody wore clogs in winter.' 'New Street! There's some big houses in New Street. Double-fronted . . .' Then, 'Ah,' she said, 'that's Water Street . . .' And so it went for a lyrical while, more shops, more streets, more names she knew, a few faces she puzzled over, the several rather grand houses proudly scrutinised . . . until she tired, rested back on her pillow and slept, replete and, John thought, as happy as he had seen her for some time.

He went out to the car to make some calls and check the emails, and read the newspaper. She would rest for an hour or so if she followed her usual pattern. He, too, could do with a nap: the drive that morning, even though he had left at six o'clock to avoid the heavier traffic, had been an unexpected slog. What had happened inside her mind when those images had painted themselves on it? Had they triggered into life areas of meaning that could be fortified by a more systematic employment of old photographs? There was growing evidence that singing old songs learned in childhood and adolescence was not only a help but a therapy and he had stumbled on that with his mother. Singing, anthropologists said, was likely to have been the origin of speech. Could old photographs perform a similar restorative function?

As he sank into a shallow drowse, he thought of Grace. She would have known that town at about the time of the cover photograph. For Mary, the photographs were potent even if they had been taken a few years before she had been born. The town had changed so little until after the Second World War. But Grace could have actually been there; Sarah could have brought her to the market. Perhaps she was the little girl in the white bonnet beside the handsome Victorian street lamp, one of four that guarded the Memorial Fountain. So Mary might just now have seen her 'own mother' as a child . . .

~

John went back in, foolishly, as he later realised, thinking that the mood he had left behind would be waiting for him on his return.

'Where've you been?' she said.

'Just outside.'

'You never come to see us.'

She looked so dramatically pitiful and her statement was so off-truth that he laughed. 'Your memory's let you down again.'

'Has it?' She rather brightened up. 'It does, now and then. It's a terrible thing growing old. Never grow old. There's nothing to be said for growing old.'

'I'm already old enough.'

'Are you? How old are you, then?'

'Seventy-one.'

'Are you seventy-one? Oh dear. What does that make me?'

'Ninety-two.'

'I'm not.'

'Ninety-two.'

'I'm not going to be ninety-two. No. I don't want to be

ninety-two. And I don't want to be a hundred. It's just a number. All the fuss they make! Ninety-two? No!'

'What age do you want to be, then?'

Mary took her time: by now the self-pity was gone and most likely erased. Such erasure could be counted a blessing, just as the everyday delight in the repeated everyday event could be a new pleasure. The lengths of absence might be compensated for by the intense present. Living just for the moment, John had read, is the purest state; it is that which mystics and meditators seek, and which, on a less elevated level, people feel they can experience by gazing at the sea, or a landscape, or the sky, or a work of art, or just being 'in the moment'. The present is always contrasted favourably with the pull and the laments from the past and the anxieties over the future. The present was the time of life and Mary had that.

But, he thought, at far too great a cost.

'Eighty-two,' she said. 'I'll be eighty-two.'

'That means you were eleven when I was born.'

'Don't be silly.'

'Never mind. Eighty-two it is.'

'Or seventy-two?'

'I don't think you'd get away with that.'

'You're right!' She waved her forefinger at him. 'I'll stick to eighty-two.'

He went to sit beside her as he had done and picked up the book of Wigton and the Solway Plain, which included not only photographs of Wigton but also of Silloth and the scattering of north plain coastal and marshland villages, including Oulton.

'Is there a dance on tonight?'

'I expect so. Somewhere or other.'

'I was thinking of going.'

'How would you get there?'

'Bike. What do you expect? Me and your dad had a tandem. It was the worst thing we ever did . . .'

'I could take you in my car,' said John.

'Have you got a car?'

'Yes.'

'Very posh. I'm not so sure about that. Where's the dance?'

'Oulton.'

'Is it far?'

'Twenty minutes. In the car.'

'Is it a dressy do?'

'Not very.'

'I'll think about it,' she said. 'I loved a dance. I loved a dance.'

'You did . . .'

Again she leaned back into the pillow and closed her eyes and, in an instant, left him.

He waited a while . . . Then she woke up.

He picked up the Wigton book and once more they riffled through it, but briefly and without the former energy.

'There were some funny people in Wigton,' she said.

'How "funny"? Made you laugh or made you worried?'

She frowned as she tried to sort it out. Finally, 'Kettler was funny,' she said, 'but he could be nasty at times. He was at my school.'

'Do you remember the prodded rug?'

'I like prodded rugs.'

'Kettler and the prodded rug. And the raffle. Do you . . .' Was it a spur, a help to use this word? '. . . do you remember?'

John knew that Mary loved stories about Wigton. The place, the community, the people had grafted themselves on

102

to her mind from childhood and with increasing intensity when she found that she had no 'real' parents, no family of her own save the town.

'Kettler . . .' She nodded. So he told her what she knew and had forgotten about Kettler.

When he had left school Kettler had worked in the coal mines a few miles from Wigton and from there gone on to the land as a labourer and had eventually been netted for the war, though not without two years of a masterful evasive strategy. He'd landed up in uniform, which he hated, in the Army, which he hated, in France, which he hated, and in battle, which he hated. When he came back he settled in Wigton, signed on for the dole, vowed to dedicate himself to drink and work as little as possible within the bounds of survival. He gathered around him a small but loyal posse of equally dedicated men, one of whom, Diddler, had inherited a couple of houses, better described as hovels, from a father who was a rag-and-bone, scrap-iron, move-anything merchant. Diddler's father, his flat cart and his grey pony combed the streets and the countryside daily and he had snapped up or, some said, just snaffled enough to invest in the hovels. Kettler had a room in one of them and promised to pay the rent one day.

His clothes were cast-offs. His food was the stale bread at the end of the day from John Johnston's bakery and bits of old meat from one of the butchers, Isaac Toppin. For both men he did a little fetching and carrying. He was always available, outside opening hours, for fetching and carrying, and the tanners and the bobs added up. Sometimes he would sub-contract to a needy boy for a promise or a penny. The big pay days were Tuesdays and Thursdays, market days, when he would stalk the auction rings from the early morning and be first in the queue to drive cattle and sheep through the town down to the railway station for export to Carlisle and beyond, or help load a truck, swill down a pen, generally make himself indispensable.

On those days the drinking money mounted up. A little more came from dominoes, which he played ceaselessly, a penny a drop, and the pennies could soon add up to a pint. He had never been known to refuse a drink. His beer was mild, the cheapest, with a half of porter if he was in funds. His great nose was ripe, corrugated, textured, pimpled and coloured beyond the dreams of Rembrandt. He managed to spend considerable time propping up a wall, usually a pub wall, in the high street or in King Street, closely observing the world going by.

He was a man to whom local legends attached themselves. To Kettler anything that was in open country was common property. Rivers were never private. Fields of turnips and potatoes were studied for their peak pinching time. There had been the matter of the rustling of sheep out in the fells. Mostly, though, tales of Kettler were exchanged to make you smile. He and his friend Diddler had dressed up for a Wigton carnival as a circus ringmaster and a wild bear. They had got hold of a bearskin and Kettler had borrowed a chain and padlock from the blacksmith. He had also, it was agreed, rather skilfully begged or borrowed an assortment of garments that made him look like a passable ringmaster. With a top hat – and a whip.

On the march through the town they were placed behind the band and Diddler had a great time rushing at the crowds, especially the children, growling and clawing the air and panting his beer-thickened breath all over them. Kettler with the whip tried in vain to keep him in order. The top hat was taken off more than it was kept on and held out for contributions, which some of the holiday crowd felt obliged to make.

When the carnival reached the middle of the town, it had swung off west at the fountain to go down a road of bungalows to the park, recently opened, built about half a mile from the old town centre. That was where the sports were held and the floats and the costumes judged. Kettler and Diddler wanted none of that. The fountain was a large memorial to the wife of a local man who, generations before, had gone to London, found it paved with gold, come back, restored a castle and, on the death of his wife, commissioned a central monument in the town to her memory. Cattle drank from it. Four gas lamps embellished it. Kettler and his friends adopted it as the forum for their daily chronicling of the town. Black railings protected it and it was to these railings that Kettler padlocked his good friend Diddler while he strolled across to the Kings Arms.

The howls of the bear were heard throughout the streets. The railings all but yielded to Diddler's fight for freedom. When asked in the pub why he had padlocked his friend, Kettler said, 'Bears dissent drink.' It became a catchphrase and for years Diddler dragged it round the pubs like a tin can tied to a dog's tail. 'Bears dissent drink, Diddler, remember?'

'Kettler and Diddler would go into the pubs on a Saturday night. With this prodded rug.' John told his mother the story, as she had once told stories to him.

'It was a very fine prodded rug. They held a raffle for it. Tickets threepence each, six tickets for a shilling and round the pubs they went on Saturday night. Everybody joined in.' She was intent – was she? 'There were about fourteen pubs in those days. Before then, before the war – I think Dad said there were twenty-nine. And the rug-raffle thrived. Every Sunday and Monday people would say, 'Who won it?' 'Oh,' Kettler would say, 'a couple from Carlisle.' The next week, 'Who won it?' 'Oh, a lad from Fletchertown, I forget his name.' And again 'Who won it . . . ?' They kept it going for about a month and then people started to notice that it was always the same prodded rug, a fine rug, and they began to say it was strange that no one they knew ever won it. People were getting very upset and just at that moment Kettler announced, in the bar of the Lion and Lamb, that they were out of prodded rugs and there would be no more raffles. 'All over!'

Mary said, to be helpful, 'Kettler would torture things – at school. Frogs.'

'I didn't know that,' said John. And he laughed. Sometimes what else could you do?

~

As he drove south he thought the fact that Mary could live more fully in the past than the present was no surprise. Time purged away the sores and diseases and impurities and left those photographs, serene and assured. And that was the time of her youth, her command of her world.

He would be like that, as he, and increasing millions, flowed in a mass slow motion towards an ever-receding death date. He would see the photographs again. He would want his own, a purged past of his own.

He was not alone. The past was already in so many ways far more attractive than the future for so many people now. 'As is, as was and ever shall be' seemed well ahead of 'As might be different'. And he was part of that.

What sort of life was it for her? That was what mattered. Who could bear it? But perhaps the photographs could not only help her but change her. Would it be possible to restore what seemed to have gone? They restored the body with surgery. The brain was part of the body. Or was it better to talk? Not a talking cure to release tension and barriers and liberate her from the past but a talking cure with a more modest aim, to be a reminder, to give her back more of her past. Or was it best left undisturbed? Would Grace's story console or upset her?

CHAPTER TWELVE

When war was declared, it changed all the world, Grace thought, except Oulton.

Some months before it started Mr Walker had given a passionate sermon, declaring that 'we' – the English, he meant – should never fight against the Germans because we *were* Germans and any clash would provoke Armageddon, or be Cain and Abel revisited. Mr Walker had a bigger agenda – his pacifism – but he had not quite the nerve to deliver it and the German issue was the nearest he could get.

He had spent a year studying in Germany and come back with a conviction that the culture and the history of that country were to be admired and copied. He brought back German words that sounded English – especially local dialect English. He gave examples of hymns they had in common. He kept referring to Martin Luther and what we owed to his 'great courage' and the Protestant Reformation, which had revealed that the true path to God was through faith and not through wealthy churches and 'corrupt illegal popes and cardinals and priests'. The greater struggle, he declared, was the fight for souls, and in that the German people, especially the Lutherans, whom he had met, were allies; the Methodists were their brothers. He was a fine figure in a pulpit, the minister. A strong face, thinning sandy hair, a leanness that worried some of the women, but a strength that showed itself when he helped at haymaking or harvest.

His voice and his manner in the pulpit were poles apart from the rather shy man about the village. The German sermon impressed even those it puzzled. For some weeks the congregation rather expected the course of events to follow Mr Walker's injunction. For not only did he bring them news from the outer world, he was a man of great biblical learning, and in some ways, and most importantly to the enthusiasts, he could get carried away by the spirit. The congregation could see the spirit in the more ecstatic hymns or towards the end of one of his apocalyptic sermons when, in measured tones but fiercely, he called down wrath and damnation on all who did not tread in the true path of the Lord. To be zealous was proof of godliness. The apostle in his passion was to be respected. Grace was impressed. The Lord was speaking through him.

Even when the war began and the propaganda portrayed the Germans as rapists and savages, Mr Walker held on for a while. But gradually he let it go. He knew from his prayers that he was right; he knew that there would be Armageddon and the world would change for ever. But although God was with him, Oulton was not. The men went off to fight. The country cheered their departure. The country believed it was fighting in a righteous cause. We were bound to win. God was on our side.

Yet even as the first grim reports came in, Grace thought over what the minister had said. She did not enter into his passion but he had made her realise that much more was at stake than just another foray across the sea with jolly songs – 'Goodbye, Dolly, I must leave you, though it breaks my heart to go . . .' Enormous forces were at work if only she could grasp them. She respected the minister.

She would linger at the graves of Belle and their mother after chapel, not only to think more on them, but in the expectation that the minister, the last to leave the chapel, would come across to talk to her. He could talk effortlessly, like no one else she had ever known. He could move from the war into a conversation about ideas and subjects Grace had never thought of or about books he had loaned her. He made everything into a conversation just between the two of them, quietly provoking her responses, often helping her along with them, teaching and nourishing her.

She came to cherish these encounters and the other times she could share his company – after a choir practice or after the Sunday school in which she taught. In these conversations she caught herself in moments of an elevated contentment unlike anything else that was happening to her, as if the branches of the trees above her in a forest had suddenly cleared and given her a glimpse of a light she had not known was there. It gave strength to her sense of independence. Mr Walker was aware of this and suffered a great happiness in that knowledge.

~

Grace became increasingly restless. Out there was the Great War, fought on land and sea and in the air. Dramatic accounts of heroism and courage came back to a troubled country. And where was she when Armageddon was heaving into full view? Stuck. Stuck in the same village doing the same things with the same people in the same way: stuck. A few regulations and directions from central government on how farmers could farm more efficiently. Little to worry about. No connection with the daily remaking of the world. Stuck.

The focus of her restlessness became Frank. It was unfair and she tried to dislodge it but it would not go. They were now in the phase of serious courting, which meant that they were cultivating some of the ordering of married life without sharing a house or a bed. It was noted approvingly that they had 'settled down'. They were a 'fine young couple'. Certain dashing signs – like the galloping of the hunters – had lost their shine for Grace and also, she suspected, for Frank. Nowadays he just wanted to exercise the horses briskly and be done with it. He gave Grace the impression that he was happy to go briskly about all his business and be done with it until . . .

Would it be much different when they married? Would it be any different at all? And this play of anticipation was becoming wearisome. They plodded along, Grace thought, plodded down the lanes and plodded alongside the river. She did her best to throw off the restlessness and told herself that she was ungrateful and foolish and that everything came to those who waited. But her patience was wearing her out.

Why did he not volunteer?

That could be at the heart of it, she thought.

She knew that farming was considered to be an essential job and in the national interest. Like coal-mining it was protected from the increasingly frantic men-raids by the leaders of the armed forces. Bodies were needed by the tens of thousands. White feathers became a fashion, taunting young men with the accusation of cowardice. 'Pals' brigades called on the close friendships of young men, 'pals' in industries and small towns, and used them to recruit *en masse*. In peacetime the upper-class generals 'beat up', that is herded up, pheasants in order to slaughter them; now they 'beat up' young men and again for slaughter. She knew that Frank and his kind were doing as much for the war effort as half the men in France . . . but. The dreaded reports came back, the drumbeats of patriotism grew louder, spread further, struck deeper. Even at the outer edge of her country, Grace felt drawn towards its centre. The pulse of war began to throb inside her, like the beginning of a fever.

And what was she doing? The work, as the minister had pointed out, of immemorial women since biblical times. She stayed at home and minded the men. Elsewhere, though, she read that young women like her were now employed in factories, they were demanding the right to vote: they were throwing off that biblical yoke. They were liberating themselves. Grace wanted to be liberated too. As the first year of bright-eyed conflict plunged into an inferno of slaughter and fear, her dissatisfaction with herself, with Frank, and with the life she led grew until it was painful It became too much to hold in.

'Why don't you join up?'

'So that's what it's been about,' said Frank.

They were walking on the path by the stream. Late Saturday afternoon. Just before Frank would go back home for what was left of the weekend.

'What's been about?'

'You've been off with the fairies lately.' He smiled and stopped and they were face to face.

'You didn't answer. Why don't you?'

'No need.'

Still he smiled and the smile annoyed her.

'They say Your Country Needs You.'

'There's all sorts of ways,' said Frank, unruffled. 'People have got to be fed. Even armies.'

'But don't you want to be with all the others?'

It was a sullen, windless day. The earth, which sloped so

evenly down to the calm sea, was overlooked by a light grey screen of cloud that would not budge or break to let in the sun. Grace was aware that she was pushing Frank and the feeling was not pleasant. She tried to leaven the moment with a mock playfulness and lightly hit him on the chest.

'You should be out there,' she said, 'shouldn't you?'

He caught her wrist, and as she raised the other arm, he caught that also. Grace was a strong woman but Frank held her easily without locking his grip, smiling still, but now with a hardness in the smile. She saw that; she saw the shadow go across his face.

'You wouldn't be thinking I was a coward, would you?'

By way of a reply, she wrestled against his grip for a few futile moments. 'What do you think?' she said, crossly.

'I'm asking you.'

'How could you think that?'

'You still haven't said.'

'. . . No. You couldn't be that . . . You couldn't be.'

He let her wrists go and she let them fall, as if lifeless.

'I've thought about it,' he said. 'All the lads have but . . . there's plenty to be done here.'

How could she shake him? Even that expression of anger had been so slight. And now it was over.

She nodded and walked on. He followed, at a distance, and it was some little statement of time before she slowed down for him to catch up. But why had he not speeded up to catch her?

~

Wilson's fingers were now clawed with arthritis. They behaved like talons: they could clutch and, collectively, grip

114

and lift, but the flexibility of fingers had gone. The arthritis was now creeping into major joints, his knees, his hips, as if a sapling were growing inside him, one that could not be rooted out or cut down.

He was still capable on the farm, though there was a steadily increasing number of jobs he could not do. He had begun to make provision. Some of the fields were let off to his sons. He no longer did the ploughing. He kept on only one hired man. Betty, a granddaughter who had just left school nearby, had been sent along by her mother to help Sarah about the house and, along the way, learn how to keep and to run a farmhouse. Grace would not be on hand for ever.

Mr Walker thought him very much the village patriarch. There was something of the Old Testament about Wilson, not a prophet, still less a king, but one who kept the faith whatever the trials sent to test him. There he sat, in his chair before a fire licking up in flames through all the seasons, the hams above him on the iron hooks nailed on to the oak beams, the glitter of plain, polished furniture about him and, in the late winter afternoon or in the evenings, the paraffin lamp on the table. Though this farm had been in place for little more than two hundred years, there was, the minister thought, something deeply ancient about it, planted as a wood is planted and just as much part of the landscape. And there was Wilson, binder twine still holding up his trousers, stockinged feet scorning slippers, pipe as often empty for comfort as full for pleasure. Wilson, white-haired now, sat as if in judgement on all about him.

But it was the minister's opinion he wanted. Every time he came he was properly fed but every time, now, he knew that Wilson was itching to question him. When the minister did draw up his chair and they sat across the fire, Wilson began, as usually now, abruptly.

'More thousands,' he said. He indicated the newspaper, neatly folded on the fender. This new daily delivery – on the minister's advice – now brought the world to him in words and pictures in a way he had never before experienced. He was addicted to it: on Sunday when he would take no newspaper, he felt the lack of it. It had transformed his life. There were times when the minister regretted having urged it on him. He had observed the decline in the old man's mobility and he saw the popular newspaper as company for him in the longer spells he would spend in his chair. It had broken a fast of reading, which (save for a few glances at the Bible and the hymn book) had lasted through most of his life. It brought news the old man constantly found startling and often unbearable.

'Thousands of young lads cut down, it says, scythed down just like corn – it's there, the corn standing up high, take a scythe to it and it's flat, cut down, like the lads. They're no more.'

The minister braced himself and took a good pull of the strong tea, brought in by Grace.

'Why does He let that happen?'

If only he could be certain in himself. But for Wilson and others like him, it was certainty they needed from him. His duty was to provide it. He was their rock. 'The Lord moves in mysterious ways,' he began.

'There's nothing mysterious about them!' said Wilson. Across the days he had been stoking up his questions for this weekly discussion. 'Mown down. And those lads that all come from the same town, those "pals" . . .'

The minister recognised the distress. He had to dig in. 'We cannot know the ways of the Lord until the Final Judgement.'

'Why can't He tell us something now? It's now we want to know it.'

116

'He is the Almighty God. Who are we to question Him?'

'Why do we say our prayers, then?'

'In our prayers we seek His guidance to make ourselves more worthy of Him.'

'We ask for things.' Wilson was not to be placated. 'We ask for peace and we ask Him to help our neighbours and ourselves – we ask all the time. Why can't we ask why He is letting this happen?'

'I trust,' said the minister, severely, 'that this sort of talk is confined to us and does not extend to the family.'

'No!'

'I am sorry but . . .' Mr Walker rallied '. . . I admit that these are difficult times for those of us who believe. We must accept that He is at times inscrutable. We may not know His full purpose.'

'How,' said Wilson, returning to what the minister recognised was a well-rehearsed line of questioning, 'how can He be All Powerful and All Good if He lets this happen? I know He *is* All Powerful and All Good – don't get me wrong – but I want you to tell me how it works.'

That was the heart of the matter. The old man, who had leaned forward, his talon hands gripped tight around the chair's arms, now sat back, tapped the pre-charged pipe and took a spill to the fire to light it.

'We are being punished,' said the minister. 'We are being punished and we are being tested.'

'What did those lads out there ever do to deserve to be punished?'

'Perhaps it was not them, but us, all of us for what we have failed to do. All the firstborn of Egypt were innocent but we know now there was a reason for that terrible massacre. He has given us life and He has given us free will but if we betray that trust then there have to be sacrifices.'

The minister's throat was dry with strain.

Wilson seemed lost behind the smoke. He said nothing. It was up to the minister.

'He wants us all to be saved. He wants us all to cleanse our souls. But we have to learn to obey Him. The rain falls on the just and the unjust alike. The vengeance of the Lord falls on the guilty and the innocent alike . . .'

'That's what I can't grasp,' said Wilson, quietly. 'When you talked about the Germans at the beginning, I had some idea what you were saying – that we were the same under the skin and it was bad, it was brother against brother, you said. I could grasp that. But this . . . those lads . . .'

The old man was so pure in his seeking. The minister no less true to himself. Nevertheless he felt his throat contract as he tried one more time.

'There is what we know and there is what we believe,' he said. 'They are different. We, you and I and the congregation, believe that there is an Almighty and forgiving God who wants to welcome all good souls to eternal life. It is not given to us to understand everything. There are things we will never know. Maybe some day, even if only on the Last Day, we will understand. But while we don't understand, we must believe. If we cease to believe we have nothing. Without belief we are worthless, just creatures like other creatures. We deny what is most precious in us. We deny the soul. And there are those who hold that view. But we, in our chapel, we hold on to the faith and the faith tells us to endure, to seek, to hope and then salvation may be delivered to us.'

Wilson said little more. He had enough to brood on. He saw that to meet the desperation there had to be a hard creed. He had to accept that at times God was not good.

~

After the funeral, Grace managed to claim a half-hour of her father's time. They went into the park and found a free bench.

Martha's illness had been long and painful. The doctor spoke of 'consumption' and later he spoke of a 'growth'. Cancer was not yet an available explanation.

'The pity was,' James said, 'she was too full of anger. She was mad with herself because she was badly, which must have made it worse. She didn't know what she was saying half the time at the end.'

He took out a cigarette. She noticed how ingrained his finger pads were with fine coal dust and nicotine. He had never carried much fat but he had grown thinner as he had aged and yet still the blue eyes, which matched her own, were lit with a flame of life that always touched her heart.

'We never got on,' Grace said. 'I'm sorry about that.'

'One of those things,' he said. 'She might have thought you were too like Ruth. She was always asking about Ruth.' He looked away. 'It's strange the influence a dead woman can have. Sometimes it was as if Ruth was there in the room with Martha and me! At times.'

Grace asked him about the arrangements. He would move out of the house, he said, and go and live with Grace's older brother, his wife and family. The younger two girls would go one each to their two older sisters by Martha's first marriage. It was all tidied up, Grace thought, and no place for her. She had come prepared to stay and look after her father for a few months at least. She accepted his plans and knew that to challenge them would be to upset him. She could mourn later.

'And my Grace,' he said to her, 'how is she, now, Grace?'

'She's well. She's very lucky.'

'Frank seems a fine lad.'

'He is.'

'And life on that farm must be sweet: hard at times but sweet. I would have given a lot to have a small farm, you know. Just one or two acres would have done. I could have worked extra for other farmers roundabout but I'd have had my own house and place and maybe a horse, maybe a pony for you children, and a vegetable garden, hens, geese, a goose for Christmas. I would have been the happiest man on God's earth, you know, with that.' He stubbed out the cigarette and smiled at her, a smile that provoked a smile. 'I like to think it could have been the saving of your mother,' he said. 'Just a few acres . . . But it was not to be.'

As Grace huddled into herself for warmth in the train that took her back to Wigton, she was still moved by his confession. He had never said that to her before. Perhaps he had never said it to anyone – wouldn't that be a privilege! But he had not got what he wanted and now it was too late.

She wanted to have a life, some time of her life, outside the invisible walls of the village, the farm, the daily tread, Frank. The clickety-click, clickety-click of the wheels on the track urged her on to a new future and yet she was aimed for the past. She went into the corridor to be alone and walked to the end of the carriage, swaying, rather off balance, and in the space between the carriages, she flung open the window and let in the gusts of cold wind from the sea. Clickety-click, got-to-get-out, clickety-click, got-to-get-out. Got to get out.

CHAPTER THIRTEEN

When Mary was up for it, he would take her into one of the two sitting rooms. Spacious, well proportioned, fitting the ambition of the place, they were walled with armchairs leaving the centre free for the passage of wheelchairs and nurses carrying trays. The midday meal and the late-afternoon meal were served in the adjoining dining room. The television was on all the time, the consensus being among the patients that it was better on than off. The volume was moderated, too much so for some for whom deafness was part of the accumulating ailments of age.

Mary had her friends and liked to be settled in a corner with them. On the good early days, there had been something of a conversation, which John observed with the pride of a father watching his child do well. Some of the women were alert, wholly *compos mentis* and happy to patch over the gaps in Mary's contributions. John was grateful for that. Apart from helping his mother, it shielded him from the responsibility of talking to her in public. He found that very difficult. He was not so vain as to think they were being observed and overheard – although they could scarcely avoid it – but he found that, outside the privacy of her room, he had nothing to say save, 'How are you?' 'Would you like a cup of tea?' and then direct her and himself to the television.

When there were only a few in the room, most of them unmoving, exhausted by this trial of survival, it could be awkward. Mary would sometimes scan the room and say loudly, 'Everybody's asleep! Just look at them.'

'No, they're not.' John could never manage more than a whisper and he also hoped, faint hope, that it would bring down the volume of his mother's proclamation by example. 'They're watching television.'

'They're asleep! And where are the men? Why are there no men?'

'There's one or two in the other sitting room. We could go there. They're in the other room.'

'I don't believe you. There's nothing but old women. It's terrible. There's nobody you can talk to!'

Mary was talking loudly to about six mostly recumbent women. It occurred to John that they were quite tactfully ignoring her.

'Oh dear.' In that phrase she almost realised what she was saying, but then she was back in the rant: 'I can't be doing with this. I'm going home.'

'Would you like some tea?' he whispered. 'I could get you some tea.'

'Home!'

'I'll see if there's any tea.' He stood up.

'Where are you going? You've just come. You never come to see us.'

He had made a misjudgement. She would be better off in her room. Mercifully he had not unloaded her from the wheelchair.

'Where are we going?'

'Back to your room.'

In the corridor, she said, 'Look at this! Isn't it marvellous? Marvellous! Look how long it is.'

122

The corridor, an impressive stretch, rarely failed to please her.

'Who lives here?'

'You do.'

'Do I?'

He took her to the end where her bedroom was located and then turned the wheelchair around and went back again and then around to feeder corridors, into dead ends that demanded a U-turn, trying, in a mood of desperate jollity, to make an event of this homeward spin. He walked fast. She liked that. He took corners pretending it was perilous. That, too, she liked. She waved at the nurses and John felt he was making too much of it, but as long as she was enjoying herself he stuck at it until he felt a sudden blanketing of depression and he steered her back into her room.

'Where's this?'

'This is where you live. Look at the photographs on the wall, and there's your dressing-gown and the fluffy toys your grandchildren bring you.'

'Have I got grandchildren?'

'Yes.'

'Aren't I lucky? I am. I am very, very lucky.' She looked out of the window. 'Look at that tree,' she said.

John sat in the chair and tried to swim out of his dark immersion. Was he helping? Earlier in the afternoon he had started to talk about Grace but stopped when her confusion began to upset her. He had been rushing it. He went outside for a cigarette and took out the letter he had received a couple of days before. It was from Mr Tate, the psychiatrist.

'Mary scored markedly better than last time on numbers,' he read. 'She was better on association as well. When I asked her who she was and where she came from she was very good. She talked a little about Wigton. She knew she was in Silloth. She remembered more of the ten objects than she had done over the last eighteen months. We are not talking about substantial but we are talking about "marked".'

What might have changed her? Were the drugs working better? Or was it the photographs, or talking to her about the Pea and Pie Supper and Kettler and the Two Wigton Mashers and dancing the Valeta?

She was becoming another person, he saw that with sorrow. She was for ever reduced to a fragment of what she had been or assuming a character he had never known her to have. That public rudeness to the other women in the room, for instance. It was totally untrue to the real character of Mary, whose politeness and sympathy for others had been set in concrete. That vulgar loudness! Where had that come from in someone who had such a sweet and rather soft voice? She would have been shocked at the vulgarity of the person she had been during those imperious moments in the sitting room. And the complaints. This was a woman whose answer to 'How are you?' was, time without number, 'No complaints! No complaints at all.'

Perhaps he was expecting too much. He smoked a final cigarette and went back in. She was watching *Singin' in the Rain*. He reminded her that the vicar would soon be round to see her. It was one of his days.

'Oh. He won't, will he?'

She looked – self-mockingly – crestfallen. But, more importantly for John, she was like her old self. He waited.

'He's a nice man,' she said, 'I like him. But . . .'

'But . . . ?'

She acted glum. Her expression was and was meant to be comical.

'He makes me feel I have to be good,' she said, and caught his eye and smiled.

She was still there! She could be reached.

CHAPTER FOURTEEN

Grace had never felt so free. The bicycle sped down the long, shallow hill, her coat flowing like a cloak, the summer dawn not long broken. She heard all about her what seemed to her to be a round of applause, in the hedges, in the fields and the trees, as strengthening light brought the awakening of freedom and the noise of greetings. She had the phrase in her head 'and the birds of the air and everything that crawled on the face of the earth' and she was at the heart of it. The village she had left behind her was stirring into labour, the horses being fed, the breakfast cooked.

But it was behind her! She was leaving it. Down she swept on the sturdily reconstituted boneshaker, pedalling hard even though there was no need, urging it on, urging herself on in this new freedom towards this new life. Life was so strong in her it could not be contained, and her body ached with it. Suddenly she shouted, then sang, loud as she could, sounds of soprano happiness, pealing across the fields, part of the waking strains of the early-morning land.

The house was no more than three miles away and once she had turned off the main road to Wigton, she found herself in narrow lanes, tunnels of trees, bulging summer hedges, flower-thickened banks, no soul stirring, no sound save for the clamour of the birds. It was like a secret passage that would suddenly reveal a great wonder, and it did.

There it stood, bold and isolated, on its own hillock as if the one were made for the other, Prospects. It was the Victorian folly of a manufacturer, Mr Birkett, who had made his fortune by industrialising the local weaving trade. In his retirement he had developed a passion for the Lake District and its many ever-changing 'prospects', the word used, he was informed, by all the best observers, for a view of nature. It was too much of a risk, too far from his business to move into the Lake District itself, but he had bought these two hundred acres of land, which included a classical late eighteenth-century Cumbrian farm on a hillock near Wigton. This was demolished and Prospects was raised up in brick and multi-gabled ambition and its prospects were satisfyingly magnificent.

It glared across the flat country to the south and on into the fells, which could be seen in intrusive close-up, thanks to a large telescope he had bought in London. An unexpected bonus to Mr Birkett was that the prospects to the north, across the sea to Scotland, were just as beguiling for some of his guests.

His granddaughter, Miss Birkett, sister of the Miss Birkett of Oulton Hall, had maintained the daunting pile – there were twenty bedrooms – for more than thirty years. She was not at all displeased to move into Oulton Hall with her younger sister and lease Prospects to the government for the convalescence of the war wounded. But she wanted to play some part in it and made that clear. One of her tasks was to recruit a good number of local women, whom she called 'my girls'. There was work to be done that mirrored what had happened in the house in its heyday: fires to be laid and lit in the mornings; heavily carpeted rooms to be kept clean

– even more essential now; the demands of the staff obeyed; the meals prepared and served. The routine that serviced the stately and the aspiring stately homes of England was largely maintained.

A hospital was bolted on. The stables were converted into operating theatres. The large drawing room was requisitioned as the principal ward. The servants were nudged out of their better quarters to make way for the qualified nurses. The issue of accommodation for staff threatened the whole project in the initial weeks. This was where Miss Birkett, spare and crisp as any military man, came into her own.

She suggested – insisted, rather, Miss Birkett always got her own way – that the general 'help' should be provided by 'girls' from nearby who could go home in the evenings and sleep there. That would save on accommodation. It would require a 'shift' system and it would mean that there had to be flexibility but Miss Birkett said that she was perfectly capable of working that out provided they left her alone.

She issued a call. Her sister helped, as did her long-time neighbour and admirer Major Eliot (Retd). Grace heard the call and was wild for it and determined to get a place. Now that Betty was there to help Sarah and the farm much reduced, she could leave at six thirty having done some chores and, due to the shift system of Miss Birkett, work from seven until four, which gave her time to get back to the farm to help clear up. Saturday hours were easier, seven until one.

Miss Birkett knew her troops. She knew and admired these strong, hardworking, generally godly, honest country girls, especially those off the farms. When the male company was a little ripe, Miss Birkett would humour them and say 'my girls know all about dealing with very demanding animals'. They were, she said, precisely what was needed and the fact that in order to accommodate their domestic imperatives the roster was impenetrable to all but Miss Birkett was neither here nor there. Miss Birkett could read the runes. It worked. Grace withdrew some of the savings Wilson had held for her and bought the boneshaker, which Frank fettled up. He even gave it a lick of new paint.

So she arrived, she thought, in high style every morning at Prospects, exhilarated by the air, slightly out of breath and, at last, part of the Great World.

~

They came to Prospects for the second stage of injury – when the major operations had been done – or for the slighter wounds. To Grace, who had never before been in a hospital, it took some time to adjust. The main thing was not to let Miss Birkett know that she ever felt queasy or helpless or nervous. 'Steady under fire' was Miss Birkett's motto.

Although her tasks were menial she was allocated a uniform, stout black shoes, black stockings, black skirt well below the knee, white blouse, one of three to be rotated so that a clean one would be worn every day. In winter there was a dark grey cardigan and at all times a white cap to tuck in hair. In the strictest privacy of her mind, Grace loved the uniform and, worse, she loved herself in it. She was serving a cause. However far she was down the ranks did not matter. The uniform was constant proof that she now had a part.

The smells could make her nauseous until her stomach found its sick legs. The suffering of some of the men and the terrible damage done to them was a drain on her affectionate heart but Miss Birkett had told them 'It does the men no good for you to be weeping willows.' She said, 'Your duty is to be cheerful at all times.' Worst were the groans and the screams. Yet the men tried to be so brave, even here where, often, it was their bravery that had brought them. They were, Grace thought, entitled to let go while they tried to mend. In the first weeks she was in a daze of admiration for every single one of them. And, mostly, just ordinary young lads, she would tell Wilson, who sat waiting every evening to hear Grace's report of her day.

There was so much for Grace to do and to learn that she thought her life could just be beginning. All the girls were from around the villages – most of whom she had never seen before. Now she had about a dozen new friends. They had much in common and yet each one was different from the next; it was perfect, Grace thought, a factory must be like this. Then, and overwhelmingly, there were the men, and the intricate range of responses between those wounded soldiers and the girls. The men liked to mock and imitate the broad accents, the local twang. The girls enjoyed that: it made them feel like a special corps and, besides, though it could be broad, their speech was plain and much more comprehensible, Miss Birkett said, than that of a Cockney or a Brummie or a Geordie. The minister, who came weekly, had told Miss Birkett that the girls spoke 'Old English'. By now he had abandoned any reference to the cousinship of the Germans but Miss Birkett took a fancy to 'Old English' and praised her girls for it.

There were the loving moments: the emotional letters that some of the men wanted to share; life stories they could not bear to keep to themselves, as if the destruction of the body had sharpened the need to feel that once they had had a life just as full as anyone else's.

At first the intensity of these encounters, the variety and

the number of them, the unhappiness, the terrible stories of the war, and yet the jokes that some men could make, often near exhausted Grace. And yet, she asked herself, as she pushed the pedals to take the bicycle up the final hill back home and into Oulton, how could she be tired? She had no right. Soon she got into the routine and she went from job to job like a bee collecting pollen, never more than a beat away from a sense of satisfaction. But even so she had to get off the bicycle and push it up the last slope of the hill into Oulton. Her new world spun dizzyingly on its axis.

~

By the following spring, Grace was thoroughly easy in the job. Most of the girls had a 'favourite' or two, although it was strictly forbidden. Some thought they were in love and secret messages were exchanged. Had Miss Birkett found out, the girl would have been put on probation and the man given a talking-to by a superior officer. But nothing could stop it and the girls could be very sly.

As spring overcame winter and the great trees on the estate began to bud, then move into heavy leaf, as the hedges regained their dense hiding places and the northern sun coaxed the first flowers into the garden and into the woods, the atmosphere shuddered with intimations of sex. Like Grace, all the girls were now at ease with their work and with the men. The schoolroom anxieties of the early months had dissolved. What they did was too important for that. They were valued, in many cases as never before, and valued publicly for helping the men to health and to fitness to go back into another battle. They began to release their sexuality in little asides and teases, between themselves at first, and then with the men, quietly, carefully, but a cat's cradle of sensuality was being made.

The men were often in a spasm of longing as the restless young women whispered about them, lowering their eyes coquettishly, pulling the white blouse tight, stroking the blanket very slowly. And then they would giggle among each other and flirt away, only to come back, a little nearer, play again, a little closer. Grace enjoyed these games, and the connection between what she was doing in Prospects and her unofficial engagement to Frank was not consciously made. They were different worlds, weren't they? There was no harm in it.

But as that spring ripened so did the desire between some of the young men and women. A hand would be caught and kissed, a breast pressed, a suggestion made that was unacceptable and rude and entirely out of bounds. It was as if Prospects had been invaded by a swarm of invisible insects full of juice and fervour, beating their wings around the faces of the flustered girls and the trapped and bedded bodies of the young men, sensing that in some cases their wounds were a source of attraction. The senior staff noticed it but could not prevent it: they, too, felt brushed by the gathering fever.

Sudden laughter would come from a distant bedroom, then silence. The girls began to give each other 'dares', some of them very hard for the sex-starved men to bear. They teased the men. There was an innocence about it, a low lean over the bed with an inadequately buttoned blouse, a fierce kiss and a promise. It began to gather a momentum of its own.

As summer came in and the windows were thrown open, and tents were pegged in the grounds as sleeping quarters for those men who were nearing the end of their stay, there were inflammatory rumours, whispered confidences, a maddening current that seized the mood of the days. It became stifling. Its intensity was unbearable.

This one is 'mine', a girl would say.

'She's for me,' a soldier would confide.

'I'll have that one.'

'That one.'

'That one.'

Grace, for a few months now, had been drawn closer to Alan. In the summer it came to the stage where she could not pass his bed without blushing. He looked out for her, and a morning without a greeting was a disappointment. She tried and succeeded in getting the job of cleaning his room – one of the bedrooms in which there were only three beds. These rooms on the second floor were the last staging post for those set to leave in a month or two. The other men there were able to get up, walk down the corridors and the stairs, make their way into the garden and leave the room to Alan and Grace. A sexual surge burst into the room when they were alone together.

She was paralysed with contradictions . . . It was wrong, this friendship, even though nothing yet had happened. But she wanted more to happen and so did he. She had told him about Frank. She had praised Frank to the skies and Alan had nodded understandingly, endorsing her high opinion of her suitor. She would talk too much – he liked to hear about the farm. He, she thought, talked too little. Yet she discovered all she needed to know, she thought.

He came from the Midlands and his father was employed in an engineering works. He showed her a photograph of his father and mother, in front of a bungalow. Another photo, of a young woman, was his sister, he said, older than he was and working as a clerk in a factory. He had joined up at seventeen, been sent to the Front a year later and had his leg badly shot up in an unsuccessful advance. There had also been some small shards of shrapnel in his head.

This information came crisp and early on and he was disinclined to dwell on it. Grace would have enjoyed more talk about the family but she saw that he was not interested. He was more interested in her life and, it seemed to Grace, he romanticised it too much.

They had read some of the same books and this, to Grace, was yet another ascent in her life. He liked to talk about them and he took her opinions seriously. Mr Walker had done that, but Alan was more personal about it, she thought, and certainly more flattering, which she rather distrusted. Most of all Alan loved poetry. 'There was this teacher,' he said, 'who made us read poetry aloud and . . . I took to it . . .' And Grace seemed to sink ever deeper into a new life.

Mr Walker, who visited Prospects regularly, saw what was happening and knew that he ought to have warned her but she was free now, released from their past. Grace met him as an old friend, a former mentor. He feared for her but her new happiness was an armour that would deflect all criticism. He prayed, though he suspected it was hopeless.

Grace came to like everything about Alan and then to love everything about him. His voice was soft and melodious, unlike any she had ever known in a man. His face was pale but sharply defined, the lips rich and strong, the eyes deeply brown, calf's eyes, she called them. He was quite tall, despite the slight stoop occasioned by the wound, and he was slim in a way she had not known that men could be slim. Just looking at him, elegant, the stick more fashionable than surgical, an open-necked shirt, a cravat, 'imitating my elders and betters: strictly "other ranks" myself,' – he enchanted her. Even the elegant way he smoked a cigarette was a pleasure to watch.

He captured her through the poetry. The lines 'Shall I compare thee to a summer's day?', 'My love is like a red, red rose', 'She walks in beauty like the night' – these were like stairways to heaven for Grace. She trusted him completely. It was in her nature to trust and his words, as he knew, sealed it. It had never in her life occurred to her that such words would be directed at her, and although she blushed and pushed him away and told him to hush, yet he persisted. His earnestness seemed proof of his sincerity. And what if he did indeed think of her in those terms? She was unbalanced by it yet in her new self she felt supported, by him, by the concentrated care he gave to her. The love – it took her an effort to say that word – that he had for her was so deep.

It was when, almost in a casual way, he said, 'When we are married,' that any doubts she had dissolved. She knew that no one could mention marriage without having given it the greatest thought. He had not yet asked her but by that casual aside he had as good as asked her and she felt herself float up to meet him in some finer place. What their life would be, where it would be, what they would do she neither knew nor cared. All the cautions of her country education were swept away by this boldness, this foreignness, this life of words and love that firmed her body and seized her mind. She avoided him for a couple of days to attempt to collect herself, which she did.

She came back to see him with questions and reservations but they were crushed by the poignancy of his desperation. Had she deserted him? Had she thought better of it? Why had she left him? In these cries she heard the sound of a role for herself. He was not omnipotent: she had power too. He needed her to live. That was what he said.

And she believed him. But her belief was not an abject thing: it gave her strength, it gave her an equality.

The meetings in his room and the few legitimate short outings in the grounds soon became restrictive. They took risks. The risks added to the excitement. They began to fumble each other, and it was then that Grace made the decisive move to tell Frank that it was over between them.

~

They went for a walk down a familiar lane. She thought it would help but the exchange was no less difficult and unhappy for that. It was Grace who began. Frank's silence had never been as crushing: she thought she might wilt. She apologised. She said that she had loved him very much but it had come to an end. She took a deep breath and said that she had met someone else – at Prospects. Was she sure? he asked. Yes, she said. She had thought about nothing else for weeks. I knew there was something, he said. He looked at her full on and she needed all her courage. I wish you wouldn't go, Grace, he said, I really wish you wouldn't go. And she wavered, as that shaft of directness, that incomparable honesty, shot into her. You're a good man, Frank, she said. She was sorry. He would find somebody else. There were a lot of girls and one of them would be very lucky to get him. But it's you I want, Grace, he said, it's only ever been you. I thought we both felt the same way. She felt, and she was right, that there was something broken in his tone, in his bearing, maybe even in his heart. She had not realised that he loved her so much. He looked forlorn. He looked sad as she had never seen him. But she managed to hold firm.

Alan, with his soft voice, the books, his poetry, the promise of a new unknown life together, his passion, made her feel that he had to be the one she could live with. It was destined. The poetry confirmed it. However hard it was on Frank, and however hard it seemed to her, it had to be done. They stood, a few feet apart, in the darkening lane, waiting as if for a miracle to give each one what they wanted without hurting the other. The bonds between them had never been so strong. Just to move seemed impossible. But it had to be done, Grace knew that, and she reached out and touched his shoulder and turned and walked back to the farm in a turmoil of grief, fear and hope.

~

Alan liked to speak the poetry aloud but he hated to do it when others were nearby. Beyond the formal gardens, they found a small, thickly wooded copse. A gentle snaking path steered you down to the stream. If you turned left then, after a few yards, you would be in an area of barely visible tracks and safe, dark concealment. They found their own glade and went there after Grace had finished her work, in the still-warm evening of the day.

Alan, who was more aware than Grace of what was to happen, was by now in a condition of desperate longing. He was convinced that he loved Grace as no one had ever loved a woman before. It was worship. He let her long black hair trail through his fingers as if it were a waterfall of pleasure. He looked at her blue eyes so intently that he might have been attempting to hypnotise her. Her body, lean, firm, made to make love, he thought, white as marble, untouched, intact, was the aching temptation to hands that could not bear to touch her, and could not bear not to touch her . . . but he could speak poetry to her.

> 'Had I the heavens' embroidered cloths,
> Enwrought with golden and silver light,
> The blue and the dim and the dark cloths
> Of night and light and the half-light,
> I would spread the cloths under your feet:
> But I, being poor, have only my dreams;
> I have spread my dreams under your feet;
> Tread softly because you tread on my dreams.'

The words wove into her soul.

They found a place, near a beech tree, the ground lush from the heat. He undressed her slowly as she lay, looking at him so trustfully – And so you can! he thought. And so you must! 'This is pure love,' he said, 'this is the union of all we can bring.'

And for both of them, physical love, though at first painful and awkward, soon felt theirs alone: no one else could have known this. Alan, whose survival and healing had moved him towards a spiritual conviction of an underlying meaning to life, and Grace, whose new poetic love had brought her to an unanticipated quality of happiness, felt that they were destined for each other. The kisses were deep. Alan's passion and the full arousal of Grace made them believe for these moments that they had in truth spread their dreams under the other's feet, and they would tread softly.

CHAPTER FIFTEEN

John and the vicar shared an old pleasure that had become a new vice. They indulged it on the beach. It was late afternoon, early autumn, a weekday, unlikely that anyone would spot the vicar and, besides, he was in civvies. To the west along the flat, sand-ribbed shore a man was speeding backwards and forwards on a motorbike between two sticks. The distance made its buzz bearable. John was gradually becoming an enemy of noise. It was a battle he lost every day. Beyond him on the shore there was a dog-walker, and a man standing stock still looking out to sea. In effect they had the beach to themselves. Hands cupped, backs to the warm west wind, they lit up and drew in deeply.

'First of the day,' the vicar said, happy to boast.

'Good going. I'm about . . . six down.' John took another extravagant puff.

'She seems settled.'

'So they say. Only lost three pounds since she came in about three years ago.'

They were walking now or, rather, sauntering not to allow mere motion to interfere with the appreciation of the cigarettes.

'They're very good there,' John added. 'I walk through the door and hear the voices of the nurses and there's

139

something . . . so hopeful and reliable about them. They're the real unsung England – they make me think about this country in ways that I thought had been buried for ever. Sorry!' He smiled. 'And it's the accent. Mine was like that once. And one or two of them have that sweet high tone that the older women used to have around here, I remember, when I was young. A singing voice.'

'Your mother still has a fine singing voice,' said the vicar. 'I've heard her singing in church. Sometimes here, they say, she'll just start it up, in that sitting room, and they'll all have a sing-song. "Come on, Mary, get us started."' The vicar enjoyed the congregational aspect of it.

'And she will,' said John. 'She'll start up. For a reserved woman she's very unselfconscious about singing. They've always sung together, that generation. I've seen the women coming out of the factory at dinnertime linking arms and singing as they walked up Station Road. You would get on a bus for a mystery trip to Silloth or Allonby or Morecambe and the singing would begin the moment the bus set off. I feel as if I'm talking to you about Merrie England and the maypole, but it happened and it happened when I was alive. Even us boys would sing on the bus when we went to play away games for the school. Rock 'n' roll, of course. Pubs had a designated room called the Singing Room then.'

'The women seem to know all the words of the old songs.'

'They'll know all the words of the old hymns as well,' said John. 'God help us, so do I.'

The mention of God seemed tactless.

The vicar fielded the problem. 'Your generation was probably the last substantial lot to go through the religious treadmill,' he said. 'School assemblies, Sunday church . . .'

'Sunday school, choir.'

'You got the full treatment. It's different now. The schools

140

are multi-faith or secular, Sunday school strictly for minors, choirs get few boys.'

'Cathedral choirs?'

'Niche!' said the vicar. 'We're quite good at niche. More cathedral choirs than the rest of Europe combined, my son tells me – he's a deacon down in Salisbury – and they seem to be pretty good. Nobody turns up to hear them, of course. The choir can outnumber the congregation.' His heel stubbed out the cigarette in the sand as if the evidence needed to be buried.

'Choral Evensong could convert a pagan,' John said.

'But to what?' said the vicar. 'Sorry. The day job.'

'Why be sorry? You believe in all that, don't you?'

'Yep.'

'The whole box of tricks?'

'The lot.'

John took out his cigarette packet and offered one. The vicar hesitated, looked at his watch, grimaced and took one.

'Get thee behind me, Satan,' said John.

'He's always in front.'

'As a boy I was a Christian fundamentalist,' said John, 'Father, Son and Holy Ghost. Virgin birth. Resurrection. Ascension. Miracles. Eternity. The Immortal Invisible. Angels and archangels. Seraphim and cherubim. Saints and martyrs. I was a zealot. I was even a crusader. Like those Islamic kids you see on television.'

'And then it drifted away.'

'Yes. All of it – it just seemed less and less credible.'

'Has anything stayed with you?'

'Well, there's a loyalty and the memory of an obsession. That's something! And, as a matter of fact, I'm back at the beginning of it. I'm tackling the first ever translation of the Bible into English for my next book. You know all this.

People then believed that the Bible told them the history of this world and revealed the next. So how can't we respect it just as a body of knowledge for so many people for such a long time? And then look at the side effects. The art, the music, the cathedrals, the churches, the language, the literature, all the social good now dismissed or derided . . .'

'Music to my ears,' said the vicar.

'You're a believer! Rare bird. Could I ask you why?'

'There's been a church of sorts in Wigton for more than nine hundred years and it's not shutting down on my watch. We've done the roof – thanks for the help. It all counts. We've done the pointing. The redecoration is under way. Now for the organ.'

'And the Word of the Lord?'

'Still there,' the vicar said. 'If you're listening. And there can be something bracing about a small band of loyalists. Christians have been few before. Who knows?'

'God?'

'You could always enquire. And maybe ye shall be answered. Ask your mother,' the vicar said. 'She could have answers. She could be in a position now to pick up some of your intimations.'

'She was christened, confirmed and married in that church.' And the unspoken sentence was: she will have her funeral there.

'They don't make them like that any more.' The vicar smiled.

'I have to go now. Carrying the torch for the death promise this afternoon. "I was dead for millions of years before I was born." Mark Twain, wasn't it? And I think he said, "And it didn't hurt a bit."'

They walked back and stopped outside the home.

'What's going to happen when everyone starts to live to be a hundred?' John asked.

'It's started already.'

'And?'

'The world will have to change. I think it might be for the better. Look what a mess the under-forties have made of it over the last few thousand years. Time for older voices who have less to gain.'

He got into his car.

'Your mother's a marvel,' he said, and then he laughed. 'She doesn't like seeing *me*! But she's very polite about it. So long!'

A neat three-point turn took him on to the ash track and on his way. John watched him for a while. It was remarkable that men like him were still around. A pity they were in the Church? Not really. Good was welcome wherever it turned up. He took out his cigarettes and made a note on the pack. 'Church organ – £250?'

~

'Hello!' she said, in a voice that made it plain she had not seen him for months but was still glad he had come to see her. He had been away for about half an hour.

'You haven't eaten much of that.'

'I've had enough.'

He assumed his usual feeder seat.

'No.' She turned her face away. 'I can't eat another thing.'

'You've scarcely touched it. Just one spoonful.' He scooped up the scrambled egg. Again she turned her face away. 'Now, no! I mean no.'

'What about a chocolate?'

'What sort?'

He picked up the box she particularly liked – a tray of

large milk chocolates, elaborately packaged. She loved them. She peered at the handsome assortment. 'There's so many,' she said. 'I've never seen so many beautiful chocolates.'

John took one while she made up her mind. When she did, she consumed it in mini-nibbles. 'Aren't they beautiful? They're beautiful.'

At this time of day there was a space of silence in the home. Tea had finished and the nurses would be busy in the kitchen and the sitting room at the other end. John studied his mother. There were a few patches of brown on her face, a rather large one on the right side of her strong nose, and her hands were a quilt of dark stains on silken, thin skin, but when she smiled or when she was merely alert, there remained that unobtrusive loveliness, he thought.

'What are we going to do, then?' She had finished the chocolate.

'You decide.'

'We could go for a walk.'

'It's a bit too dark.'

She shook her forefinger at him. 'You're right. Too dark . . . We could go home.'

'Not today. Maybe soon.'

'Why not today?'

'You can't walk properly.'

Again the wagging finger. 'That's true.'

'We could sing,' he suggested.

'We could,' she said. 'Nobody'll stop us.'

'What'll it be?'

She began:

> 'If I were the only girl in the world
> And you were the only boy
> Nothing else would matter . . .'

'Not that.'

'Why not that?'

'It can make me a bit weepy,' said John.

'You're soft,' she said. 'Soft.'

'What about "My Bonnie Lies Over the Ocean"?'

'That has a good tune,' she said, and immediately began:

> 'My bonnie lies over the ocean.
> My bonnie lies over the sea.
> My bonnie lies over the ocean.
> Oh bring back my bonnie to me.'

He joined in:

> 'Bring back, bring back,
> Oh bring back my bonnie to me,
> To me.
> Bring back, bring back,
> Oh bring back my bonnie to me.'

This was the way the world should end, he thought. This was the way the world should end, not with a bang, not with a whimper, but with a song.

> 'Oh bring back my bonnie to me.'

CHAPTER SIXTEEN

He wrote the day he arrived home and his second letter was inside a package in which were two books: there was a volume of Shakespeare's sonnets with the line 'Shall I compare thee to a summer's day?' specially marked out, and there was a slim collection of W. B. Yeats with a whole poem outlined in black ink and the last line underscored in red: 'Tread softly because you tread on my dreams.'

Grace was a little self-conscious of her own letters but Alan's compliments reassured her. Miss Errington had picked her out for composition. She kept him up to date with notes on life in Prospects. Miss Birkett had tightened discipline and three of the men had been given a dressing-down. Prospects might close now that the war was coming towards its end, now that the Americans had joined in. She often went down the path to 'their' place. She missed him and (after rejecting 'best wishes' and 'kindest regards') managed, at first with some difficulty, to write 'Much love, Grace'.

Alan's letters flamed like his talk. His handwriting was as loose as hers was steady. His sloped from left to right and at the bottom part of the page was almost crammed into the corner. She could always rely on a few lines of poetry. He wrote little about his family but then neither did Grace.

He'd had to go into a local military hospital for a final check-up but he would soon be out and fit as a fiddle.

And so they batted their feelings backwards and forwards for a few weeks. Sarah was impressed by the regularity of the letters. Wilson had withdrawn from all participation in the matter. He was disturbed by the ending of what for him had been a very public though informal engagement with Frank. He did not know this other man and he was perturbed that the soldier had not managed to come to the farm to make himself known. What sort of a man was that? And Grace had altered in a way he did not like. What sort of a woman just changed her mind for a stranger and one who showed no respect or any sense of honour? She was somehow off the ground, head in the air, in danger of losing herself.

Sarah encouraged Grace to talk about Alan but it did not add up to very much. It was all a bit sudden, Sarah thought, and 'all a bit sudden' meant not good. Sudden was danger. Sudden was unprepared. Sudden was to be avoided. 'All a bit sudden' was worrying, although it was better not to say so.

Grace was a little puzzled that Alan had proposed no plan. She thought he might have invited her to go and stay with his parents. She had already imagined the train journeys through half of England. The soldiers, she had heard, were crowded on to the trains; the uniforms and talk of war, the smoke and the noise, this was the real world. She knew it was a time of unhappiness and horror for so many and she tried to sympathise with that and, faced with an example of it, she would have helped in any way she could. But in the exhilaration of this new kind of love and in the new feeling of being unbound, she saw the opportunity to leave Oulton and go deep into the heart of England as a chance for freedom. He would summon her in good time, she was sure of that. But she began to sicken for him.

Then came the letter that devastated her.

Dear Grace,

I am Alan's father. He's told me a lot about you, all of it good. You sound like a fine girl and I know he is fond of you. I write to tell you that when he went away for a final check-up they found that the shrapnel in his head had not been removed, that is to say not all of it, and complications have set in. He has to be kept in a restful state with no excitement. It is not touch and go as they say but it does not look too bright on the horizon.

Added to the above, I am sure you know that Alan is a lad with his head in the clouds. He has always been a bit of a romancer. He was always inclined for that sort of thing. My wife (Elsie) has taken the liberty (given the circumstances and wanting all the information we could get to help him) of looking at one or two of your lovely letters and as we suspected he seems to have made promises he just can't keep. He is in no condition to do so and the doctors say he likely never will be.

This is a hard letter to write but both Elsie and myself agree it will be an even harder letter to read. Of course we cannot force you not to write to him but this is just to say that we won't be sending on the letters to him for a while unless he asks about you. But he is in a world of his own at the moment, Grace, and that's the truth of it.

If you would allow Alan's father and mother to give you some helpful advice, it would be to try to get over him and find somebody else worthy of all the good things he said about you.

I am very sorry to be the bearer of this news.
Yours sincerely,
Alfred Marshall

She remembered Alan's moments of desperation and wanted to rush to his bedside, just to be there for him. Yet his parents had all but banned it. She wanted to write a letter every day, but would he ever read it? Instead, after two days of crushing indecision, she wrote a brief, affectionate, but essentially passionless letter to his parents who would, she thought, be worried enough without having her worries to cope with as well. At times through those days she felt that she was being choked and had to stop whatever she was doing and order herself to be calm and breathe deeply and regularly and avoid the piercing glance of Miss Birkett and the enveloping concern of Sarah, who knew that something bad had happened and was certain it had been in that last letter. The handwriting was unknown to her, which made it even more upsetting.

Grace simply did not know what to do with herself. She did not know where to put this thing that was her body. When she came home from the hospital she felt relieved at the private familiarity of it after what she feared had been the transparency of her feelings at Prospects. But soon the brief moment of peace would pass. She would go out into the fields, down the paths, anywhere to be alone. Yet when alone she was not wholly aware of who she was and what she was, now, alone. Her skin crawled with agitation as if it longed to be sloughed off. What did it mean – 'he had always been a bit of a romancer'?

Alan was gone. That was the truth of it, wasn't it? He was lost to her. She had said in her letter she would 'wait for him to get better' but by return Alfred had told her that it would be 'fruitless'. He was very sorry. Alan was going to take a long time to mend; the doctors said he could even get worse.

But Grace did not mind that! She wanted to be with him so much. She would look after him. She would spend her life looking after him. They loved each other. What could be better than being with the man she loved and what did it matter that he was ill and getting more ill? He would need her more. Did they not realise how much she and Alan loved each other?

I know you are being very kind. But I have to say that Alan and I loved each other in a very special way. I don't mind how ill he is. I am more than happy to spend my life with him, as a companion, as a good friend, just to be near him. I know he very much wants me to be near him. He told me that and I want to be near him. I will take care of myself. I am sure there are jobs available. I don't mind hard work. But please, Mr and Mrs Marshall, will you let me come and see him at least and then maybe we can go on from there? There is nothing else in my life I want more than to be with Alan.

She had posted it as soon as she had finished it so as not to have time to rewrite it and moderate the strength of feeling that she feared might unnerve them. It did.

Dear Grace,
It is with great regret that I have to bring this correspondence to a close. My principal duty – and that of his mother – is to Alan. He needs peace and quiet and no disturbances of any kind at all. Be assured that Elsie and myself go and see him on a regular basis and make

sure that everything is being done that can be done. I am truly sorry that it has turned out like this but I think it would be unfair of me in any way to keep alive any hopes you might have. So I sign off now, wishing you all the best in the life you have ahead of you.

Yours sincerely,

Alfred Marshall

It was soon after receiving that letter that she admitted, to Sarah, that she was pregnant.

~

She sank down to the dark seabed of her self where consciousness only flickers and the unconscious is peopled with silent, shadowy, fearsome creatures of harm. She lay in her bed like a corpse. Sarah had to feed her one or two spoonfuls of soup at a time. Her eyes, so keen, so sharp and lively, were glazed in such sorrow that Sarah could scarcely bear to look. Grace had lost herself.

Wilson was almost as unmoving as Grace. He had taken the news badly. He felt betrayed, a feeling new to him and all but unbearable. Sarah made some excuse about the young man being taken ill again and Grace being dissuaded from seeing him but Wilson knew. He knew that the man was a scoundrel and if he had still been in Prospects Wilson would have gone down there and taken the whip to him, wounded hero or no wounded hero. He had blighted Grace's life and skipped off, and now he was refusing to take responsibility. There was not a word in Wilson's spoken vocabulary black enough to describe that.

But, to Sarah's grief, Wilson took against Grace. She had

conducted herself so well with Frank, and he such a fine man. Now, this soldier boy had turned her head and she had given up her virginity to him, a stranger. It was not the Grace he knew; not the Grace he had watched and delighted in. This was not the Grace he wanted under his roof.

'You must let her stay at least until she has delivered the child,' Mr Walker told him. 'This is your minister talking, and I am advising you to do this for Christian reasons.'

The old man, now almost sunk into himself, stared at the preacher and offered no response.

'We have to learn to forgive,' said the minister, 'especially to forgive those we love. We will soon be asked to forgive our Great Enemy in War and many of us will find that hard but we will do it. How much more important, then, to forgive those nearest to us? You cannot put the girl out of your house, Mr Carrick. I will not let you lose your conscience in this matter.' Mr Walker would not be challenged on this.

The old man would not reply.

'The chapel will pray for you,' Mr Walker said to Grace, in the attic bedroom.

'No,' she said quietly, rather hoarsely, but emphatically. 'No. No. I want no prayers in the chapel.'

'But the congregation wants to help you.'

'No. Most of them think it's my own fault and it will be more than I can bear.' For once, in days, she was animated. Her eyes fastened on his sympathetic gaze. 'Promise me. Please. No prayers, no sermons. Nothing. That's the least I can hope for. Nothing. Please!'

'Her earnestness,' he said to Sarah, 'a better word is passion, though I hesitate to use it, is compelling. There is something quite frantic about it. I fear that if I disobey her it will make her even more ill. And yet, Mrs Carrick, it is her duty to obey me.'

'I'm going along with her,' Sarah replied. 'I think that doing nothing's the best course.'

He nodded. 'I'll call again tomorrow.'

It was as much as people could do not to call. Gossip was a substitute. What a fall it was for Grace, so lovely, so clever, so fine and natural! Frank, some said, was well out of it; others blamed him for not being the man and going down to that Prospects place and sorting the soldier out. But that was Frank: you couldn't ruffle him. And the soldier, they said, had run away, or he was dying, or he'd gone back to the Front. Whatever it was, it was a terrible shame, and a shame on Grace, many thought, that would never be washed away. She ought to have known better. She did know better and yet look what she had let happen. Girls less clever and pretty than her had not fallen into that trap. It was a side of her that some had never suspected but a few declared they had seen it coming all along.

~

Miss Birkett – of Prospects – arrived in style on her grey mare. The hired man, drawn to the farmyard by the clatter, took the horse like a groom and Miss Birkett entered the farmhouse.

Wilson was in the garden. Sarah was stacking logs by the fire. Miss Birkett put out her right hand and Sarah, having wiped her own, took the firm handshake and indicated a chair.

'A perfect farm living room, Mrs Carrick.' She looked around with an auctioneer's bold stare. 'Not a thing out of place!'

'Thank you . . . I was about to make some tea.'

'That would be marvellous. Can I see Grace while you're doing that?'

'. . . Yes. I'll take you up the stairs.'

Miss Birkett, rather military in her fitness and her precise movements, was a little forbidding, no doubt the lady, Sarah thought, but there was a warmth she trusted. She pointed towards a chair by the bed and left the two of them together. Miss Birkett noticed that there was a copy of Shakespeare's sonnets on the bed, lying within reach. It never did to underestimate these young country women.

Grace wished she had not come.

'I hope you don't mind,' Miss Birkett began, in a softer tone than Grace had heard her employ.

Grace gave no response. She saw the ruddy sheen on the finely drawn face, the bundle of grey hair hastily knotted to fit under the riding cap, which she had left on the downstairs table. She heard a kindness she had not heard before.

'You must be very tired and very upset. You couldn't be better cared for.' She glanced around. 'What a pretty room. I should have brought some flowers.'

Grace's resignation thawed a little.

'I won't tire you further, Grace. I hope you don't mind – I've said that, haven't I?' She laughed. 'I must be a little nervous!'

Why? Grace was puzzled.

'I have three points to make. I even put them on a piece of paper.' She fumbled in her deep pocket and then said, 'I don't need it . . . I feel responsible, Grace. You were under my care. You were one of my brighter girls! It was my responsibility to make sure you were safe and I failed. I ought to have spotted what was going on. I ought to have nipped it in the bud. I will not forgive myself.'

Grace made a gesture that indicated forgiveness.

'No, no. I failed.' She took a deep breath. 'Right. Grace. I want to tell you something. What has happened to you has happened to other people before. I know this to be true.' She paused, she hesitated, she considered. Then she went on, 'And while the world wants to cast the first stone, there are those of us who can understand. Those of us who can sympathise. You are *not* a bad person, Grace. You are a fine young woman. What has happened is unfortunate and I believe the young man is . . .' (evading his responsibilities? Miss Birkett had heard that he had been involved in a similar incident at the previous hospital – she ought to have known that! But this was not the time to say it. There would not be a time, she decided there and then, there would not be any time to say it or to countenance it being said) '. . . back in hospital. Some of these young men have suffered too much.'

Grace nodded. This was true. Alan had suffered too much.

'But you are not on your own,' the visitor said, her ramrod back having moved not an inch in a speech that was taking more out of her than she had anticipated. 'There are those who will help you and I am one of them. There is nothing you need say or do now. But when you do need help I will be at your side. Now, I must leave you to rest . . .' She would impart the gist of this to Mrs Carrick.

Miss Birkett went to the home of her sister nearby. The Hall was a modest seventeenth-century house that had somehow survived the indigence of a succession of squires to be snapped up by the owner of Prospects. The sisters were on close terms. She knew that her semi-reclusive younger sister would want to know every detail, not for gossip, for a sort of comfort.

~

When Grace got the strength and the will to leave the house she chose the quieter walks but wherever she stepped she felt a tremor beneath her feet. She had read *The Scarlet Letter* and now she lived it. The minister was to move to another chapel. It was time for a change, he had told Grace, but, through Betty who was proving a reliable young carrier of gossip, he had been asked to move because he 'went on and on about how everybody had to forgive their enemies and that meant you as well as the Germans. They said he went on about you too much,' said Betty. Betty did not need to add that many of the Primitive Methodists looked on Grace as a fallen woman and a blemish on their chapel and were not forgiving. The minister's attitude had fired their obstinacy with one especially challenging sermon and from then on the line was drawn.

So Grace walked, she felt, in shame. But walk she must. The doctor had told her that lack of air and exercise would endanger the health of the child. Just as she must eat properly: she was not one now, he said, but two. Grace grasped that immediately and set herself to do as she was bid. But every encounter along the walk was a trial. The quieter walks seemed to be more populated than usual. And every passing neighbour released another surge of shame.

Were they only saying little beyond 'Hello' because they were shy and kind? Or because they were condemning her with the meanest portion of speech they could utter? Two of them said nothing at all and Grace felt cut to the heart. She had known these people all her life. She lasted about fifteen minutes of the first day and when she got back to the farm, feeling drained of life beyond her understanding, she went to her bedroom and longed for Belle to be there, to hold, to talk to.

But there was no lack of courage in her and the next day

she went out again. And the next. And continued every day but Sunday when she never left the farm. Although two or three people were determinedly sympathetic, most had cast her as the fallen woman. A few enjoyed her humiliation. But her health stabilised; the weeks of sickness passed by, the child inside her grew larger, more visible, more consuming even, a companion on the walks.

There was an evening when she took a longer walk and met Frank. He had left the village and returned to his home farm but twice a week he would cycle through and exercise Miss Birkett's hunters. As Grace usually took her walk in the morning, they had never met. Now, though, as spring came through, she would go out twice a day.

He rode towards her, high on the lead horse, the second on the rein behind him. She stepped aside to give him a through way. She felt so suddenly dizzy she thought she might faint.

He stopped and looked down on her. The same calm look. The same Frank. Everything seemed the same except her, except them, except the life that would now not be lived, the path that had not been taken.

What Frank saw was a face he still loved, just a little plumper now but every bit as fine, he thought, the milkmaid complexion even more emphasised and the lushness of the silky black hair, abundant, bundled into a crown. And then his eyes dropped and he saw the pregnancy and Grace knew that he saw it and that the unborn child would be for ever too much for him. Besides, she said, in this instant conversation with herself, she loved Alan; she would always love Alan whatever happened. But then Frank looked at her again in that safe, calm way, that old certainty of promise.

'Bearing up?' he asked.

'Yes. Oh, yes. You?'

'Yes. There's always plenty of work.'

'How's Miss Birkett?' To say something; to keep him there; to say anything.

'Quiet as ever. I don't know why she keeps the horses . . .'

'And . . .' But she was done. She ached with a sadness she did not want to know. She gestured. Frank nodded and touched the flanks of his horse with his heels.

'Walk on,' he said.

And they walked on. And she looked after him and saw the riderless horse quietly, obediently, following Frank as he wended his way down the lane and he did not look back.

~

Worst of all was her grandfather. Wilson would not say a word to her. Grace could scarcely bear his silence. She spent as little time as possible in his company but there were meal-times and times when she was helping Sarah and Betty. He was not nasty about it but he never once addressed a direct word to her. She was barred from all affection and all kindness. She sorrowed for him in her bed. But she could see him in the dark of her room, bound in ice beside the fire, waiting only for her to be gone from under his roof.

~

It was a difficult birth. Grace was unable to feed the child, who was taken away to a neighbour who was a wet nurse. Her absence made Grace's condition even worse but 'she would survive', said the doctor. 'All she needs is time and help, which I know she'll get here.' And so she did, from

Sarah and Betty, but the judgement of Wilson would not be tempered with mercy. When she was well enough, she would leave his house. Grace was aware of conversations with Miss Birkett. She so longed for her grandfather to come and see her in her bedroom. Just to stand there at the door would do. She was in a terrible depth of confusion, unhappiness and pain. She wished it had been a boy and looked like Alan. She wanted the name 'Ruth', her mother's, but Sarah said that Wilson would not allow that. The child was called Mary.

CHAPTER SEVENTEEN

Mary lay on her side coiled in the foetal position as helpless as a child. He watched over her. Was he watching over an invalid? Yes. Was she in pain, or imminent danger? No. Was her illness curable? Not in her time. The problem would be solved too late for her. Too late for him, too. Knowledge was not moving fast enough for the increasing mass of the already very old. They were a new phenomenon. Only now were groups of researchers concentrating their energies on the afflictions of age.

John had sought out an acquaintance who was up to speed on these researches. It was research or mass euthanasia and most likely culling, she said. 'We are too many.' She had told him that any solution was some way off, that by 2050 between two and three million people in the UK alone would be suffering from Alzheimer's or allied diseases and that it was a crisis in waiting. Her own mother was suffering the beginnings of it – she was lucky that it had been spotted so soon. Many times it was hidden with conscious or unconscious cunning, she said. Who wanted to admit to it? There was a shame about it as there was about all diseases that seemed to be visited on the weak. There was a new drug that might slow it down but perhaps his mother was too far gone . . .

And, this fanatically fit middle-aged academic had added, however hard you tried to fight it, however many workouts at the gym and cryptic crosswords and five helpings of fruit and vegetables a day and, of course, no smoking, meagre drinking, minimal meat, regular sex, six-monthly total check-ups, no coffee and five walnuts for breakfast, it could still strike. Later, possibly, but if, as could well be, it was genetically embedded, then when it saw the opening, it would seize it.

'My husband's mother had vascular dementia,' she said, 'just like yours.' It was now quite a regular feature of John's life that he would encounter someone who was related or close to a sufferer from a form of dementia. John said that he had found singing helped. 'Scientifically proven,' she replied. 'It's very interesting how songs can be recalled *in toto* when everything else has gone. But what also works, my husband has found, is to take her back to her childhood or any other vivid times and help her describe them and tell her how good her life was.'

Afterwards John wondered whether he was doing enough about his own mother's childhood. Putting together the story of Grace and telling her about it might be a help. But there must be other ways.

He was aware of a fatigue inside his determination. By the time he got to his mother's bedside from London he would often be tired – the drive, a heavy week, deadlines over the weekend, the usual excuses. But he had to admit he could feel a helplessness, often enough to deplete his effort, even perhaps to infect her with his lack of will. When his children occasionally made the journey they would almost invariably return with bubbly news – and there was no reason to disbelieve them. He had been there with them from time to time, and what did they do? They just seemed to chat away. No agenda. Lots of compliments. Laughter. Happy noise. Teasing. She loved it. She loved it all. 'I'm very lucky with my grandchildren,' she would repeat. 'Very, very lucky! I'm very, very lucky with my grandchildren!'

He could not be them. But he saw her more frequently than they did and yet he could . . . What was the damning phrase schoolteachers used about poor performance in termly reports? – 'Could try harder'.

He watched her eyes flicker. Was her sleep the same sort of sleep as that of a baby? That was supposed to be dream-less, but was it? Perhaps her mind was like a child's and floated through new worlds in scarlet and gold, in Persian dyes and sunset pastels, and all the dazzle of an Arabian mosaic – a world in waiting, with sweet scents and sounds, a womb of mind, a rich almost-consciousness, clouds of glory, a private paradise forever longed-for? Or was she in the derelict waste of the world's end, her own world's end, with the deep draw of a drugged blank future pulling her into its open jaws? Of what was she aware? Or was it more of a blank slate, as it had been at the beginning of life, but here a clos-ing down, the lights going out, one by one by one until there would be none?

He read. It was difficult to concentrate on a book, let alone be taken over by a novel, so he read newspapers and magazines – sensible articles with a brisk beginning, a clear argument, and a firm conclusion confidently ordering wholly comprehensible worlds. A parallel fantasy, he thought, to the inscrutable dreams of his mother.

~

'Are you here?'

'Yes.' He put down the magazine and leaned forward to pick up the two-handled pink plastic baby-cup, which held the water. She grasped it with both hands. She took two small bird sips as he tipped up the bottom of the beaker. Her voice was slurred, almost a gurgle, as it tended to be when she woke up.

'When are we going out?'

'Soon.'

'That's good.' She leaned forward for another sip, then turned her face away as if he were forcing it on her against her will.

He dived in.

'Did you ever go to Prospects when you were a little girl? It was a very big house.'

'Miss Birkett,' said Mary, and she smiled. 'There were two Miss Birketts! My one had the biggest house there was.'

'Prospects?'

'She was very nice to me, Miss Birkett. Every now and then a man came in a smart pony and trap and took me away for the day to see Miss Birkett.'

'Came where?'

'Who?'

'The man with the pony and trap.'

'The house. Where do you think?'

Could she go any further?

'Whose house?'

'Our house. I loved that pony and trap. You were so proud, you wouldn't have called the Queen your aunt. And I loved that little pony. Toby. He was called Toby. Trot-trot-trot.' Her hands took the reins. 'He pretended to let me drive.'

'What did you do when you got there?'

'I played. I watched the peacocks.'

'Did you see Miss Birkett?'

'She was very nice to me, Miss Birkett.'

She lay back on her pillow and John assumed she was now in a memory-dream of the magical childhood visits. Plucked from the congested slum centre of the crammed town and whisked away through the lanes to this palace of Prospects – what could there be but good memories? He left her in peace. So Miss Birkett had carried through to the next generation. He did not want to ask her more about Prospects. He did not want her to say, 'Where?'

~

A few weeks later, on the same track, he asked, 'Do you remember Greenways?'

'Mrs Pemberton!'

'That's right. You liked working there.'

'I loved it! What a beautiful house. Beautiful!'

'We enjoyed going there, didn't we? You would plonk me on that little seat you'd had put in front of the handlebars – or when I got older on the pillion at the back – and off we would go to Greenways.'

'It had two staircases.'

'Good for games. With Lucy and Arthur.'

'They were nice children. You could all play together.'

He remembered some of that sharply. Lucy was a couple of years older than he was – about ten; Arthur a year younger than him. Lucy had a beauty John had not come across before: a tangled mane of auburn hair, speckled eyes, something – to John – magnetic about the charm and fun and loveliness of her. Arthur, too, had that look. His mother had been told they looked like their father, who had been killed in the war. In the barn they jumped from high stacked bales on to mattresses of straw. They played hide and seek all around the farm and in the house if it was raining. Mrs Pemberton seemed not to mind the noise they made, the mud they brought in, the rough-and-tumble of it all.

Lucy and Arthur went to the same primary school as John and would stay there until one day, as if a clock had struck midnight, they were spirited away to boarding-schools. John had a moon-calf devotion to Lucy and spent most of his time working out, with some success, games (like going away to war and coming back again) that had a kiss of reward at the end of them.

'Did you like cleaning?'

'It didn't bother me. Not with nice people like Mrs Pemberton.'

'Were some of the others not so nice?'

'Not so nice. Not so nice.'

John had a view that his mother actually enjoyed the cleaning and embellishment of Mrs Pemberton's house. She never complained. In the photographic album of his memory, he saw her polishing the big dining table and imagined her humming to herself as she did it. There was a complete lack of envy. But there was also, quietly expressed, an intransigent sense of equality. She played her part, just as Mrs Pemberton did. She knew, as the richer, socially grander woman did, that an appreciation of the other's nature was what mattered. Was he being romantic or sentimental? He thought not. He had seen them together later, some way down the years, Mrs Pemberton rather more the worse for wear than his mother, and seen two women walking along a cliff path arm in arm, still comfortable in each other's company, before retiring to Mrs

Pemberton's seaside villa in which John and his mother spent a short holiday.

~

He rang up a couple of days later. They would always put him through to the staff nurse on duty.

'She's taken to her bed!' There was a lilt of laughter in the comment. 'She woke up and had a look at the weather and just didn't fancy it.'

'Is she eating much?'

'We got a bit of breakfast into her. But she wouldn't touch her dinner. We'll try again at teatime.'

'But she's all right?'

'Oh, yes. She's just a frail old lady. There's days and days.' And on some days, he knew, she could be very angry, refuse her food, refuse to be washed or dressed, flail all about her. 'She has her bad days,' the nurse said, 'but if we leave her and come back later, odds are she'll be right as rain.' But it was getting worse, this resistance.

At present she had a chest infection, which took a fortnight to clear and the nurse advised him not to visit – she was asleep practically all the time.

When he did return, he breezed in, less circumspect than usual, the familiar gift – a box of milk chocolates – and flowers. She looked distracted and fierce.

'What are you doing here?'

'I came to see you.'

'Well. You've seen me.'

'I came to say hello.'

'Hello. So that's over with. You can go now.'

'They're bringing a vase for the flowers.'

'So that's done. Ta-ra.'

'What about these chocolates? Should I open the box?'

'No.' She turned into her pillow.

'They said that I ... you've been ill ... needn't come for ... until you were a bit better.' But why was he excusing himself? How could she remember his entrances and his exits? Yet guilt boiled up. 'But when I phoned they told me you were getting better.'

Her silence was unbearable this time. Usually he could bear it. On this hot afternoon, with the slap in the face of 'You can go now', he had to dig in. Maybe three score years and ten *was* enough as the Bible said. Today he felt how he was ageing too.

'I could read to you,' he said.

'What would you read?'

'The *Cumberland News* ... No? I could tell you stories you told me – "Little Red Riding Hood"?'

'Don't be so daft.'

That was better.

'"Goldilocks and the Three Bears"?'

'I know that one. I know both of them.'

'What about poetry?'

'What poetry?'

'"Daffodils".'

'Go on then.'

She was still turned away from him.

'I wandered lonely as a cloud [he began],
That floats on high o'er vales and hills.
When all at once I saw a crowd ...'

'... A host, of golden daffodils, [she said, and went on]
Beside the lake, beneath the trees, [she sat up]
Fluttering and dancing in the breeze ...

. . . Ten thousand saw I at a glance
Tossing their heads in sprightly dance . . .'

'We learned that by heart at school. It was my favourite.'
Now alert, she added, 'Grace liked poetry. She brought you
a book of poetry now and then.'

Where were they? So many moves, so much 'thrown out'
along the way. Which books had she brought him? Had she
written in them? What had she said?

He opened his briefcase. 'I've been writing about Grace,'
he said. 'Would you like to hear it?'

'Oh, yes.' She was eager now. 'About Grace?'

'Yes.' He sat down, the pages to hand.

'I'd like that. I'd like that . . .'

He began to read.

CHAPTER EIGHTEEN

He met her at the station and was glad of it when he saw the uncharacteristically tentative way in which Grace stepped out of the train and peered around as if for support. Yet as he walked towards her and she was more fully in view, he felt a smile of admiration push through his lips. What a fine young woman his daughter was! What age would she be? Twenty-one? And there she stood, taller than most of the women, still quite slim, almost proud-looking in a nervous way, a match for anybody, he thought, and just like her mother. It was the dramatic contrast between the blackness of the hair, the marble skin and the eyes. And the smile, of course. That was always where you could tell about a person, his father had said, in the smile. The seed of attractiveness was always in the smile, and if you could trust the smile then you could trust all that lay behind it. Grace thought the same about her father's smile.

They gave each other a brief, embarrassed almost-hug, then Grace linked his arm like a sister. 'I thought I would take you to Lowther's,' she said.

'Too posh for me.'

'I knew you'd say that! But there's that tea room just opposite . . .'

'Forster's.'

'Is that acceptable?' she asked, teasing him just a little, excited to be with her father.

'That would be grand.' He stopped. They were about to leave the station. 'I'm so pleased to see you, Grace. I am.'

She nodded. It took very little to move her to tears these days. He squeezed her arm, and their delight in each other's proximity was obvious to anyone with eyes to see as they walked into the middle of the thriving Georgian mining town.

'I'm sorry about the last time,' she said, as they sat at a table located in a quiet corner of the large, rather bare but well-frequented refreshment room.

'You were in a bit of a state.'

'You'd come all the way to see me.' He had arrived in Oulton like a Praetorian guard – to give visibility to his unquestioning support of his daughter.

'And see you I did. And I'm looking at you now and thinking what a fine young woman you are and I hope there are people about the street who'll see us and say, "How did that lucky devil get to link arms with a beauty like that?"'

'They'll certainly see I'm your daughter.' Grace was proud of their similarity.

'They will. Now then. Let's tackle this agenda.' He picked up the menu.

After the first cup had been drunk and the teacakes tasted and the family notices delivered, he said, 'Has anything changed?'

Grace drew a deep breath. Her choice of a public place was deliberate but she wanted no more of the quayside or park benches. It would be impossible to have a private conversation at the house where he lived. There was the Anglican church – she had thought of that – but it would be too oppressive, she thought, and, besides, would it be

172

appropriate? The Lowther, the grandest tea room in the town, had been part of it, partly a way to thank her father and partly because she thought they would be ignored there. But Forster's tea rooms was where she had expected to land up. She must not let him down. It was her first venture into any sort of public arena. She could not have done it in Wigton, where she would have felt surrounded by the over-knowing or the over-curious. But she had to start somewhere. She could not hide away for ever.

'Not much,' she said. 'One thing.'

After the child had been with the wet nurse she had been placed with a foster-mother, Mrs Johnston, in Wigton. She had two boys of her own and had fostered before, and she was currently fostering one other child. She had room, she said, in the rather commodious house bought by the council from a bankrupt estate agent. The arrangement was swiftly agreed on. Sarah would pay for the first few weeks, then Grace would take up the burden. She would be on a wage by then and there were her savings over the years, plumped out by the sale of those lambs, every penny accounted for and returned via Sarah from Wilson.

Through Miss Birkett's connections, Grace had found refuge and employment in the house of a solicitor in the south of the county, in the village of Grasmere. There was a rise in the land, a hill called Dunmail Raise, just before you went down south into Grasmere. It had once marked the boundary line of the kings of Scotland and there was still a sense of cut-off, of the land south being a different country, far from the bloodied plains, the fortified churches and houses and castles, and the foreign intervention of the great Roman wall. Gossip, Miss Birkett rightly guessed, would not reach so far and would not go over Dunmail Raise unless deliberately and maliciously carried. The solicitor and his wife would seal their lips; the live-out maid and the part-time gardener would not be informed of Grace's past. Grace would be as safe as anywhere she could be while yet being within travelling distance of the child.

Mary did not yet seem to be 'her' child. Grace's life had been organised out of it. Well and thoughtfully organised, sensibly and conscientiously organised, but it was as if she, Grace, the mother, was not a mother but a movable factor in a grander equation. In her physical weakness in the early stages she had had a resigned acceptance, which might have been the oil on the storm of pain that ripped through her. But now that she had recovered physically . . .

'So I asked for a full day off on the Saturday and caught the bus to Wigton . . .' she told her father. She wanted to tell him everything. There had to be someone who knew every-thing about her. It was a journey of about two hours with a change at Keswick. It was a trip furnished with views of memory-staining countryside, mountains, lakes, stone walls, waterfalls, woods steeped in early-autumn ripeness, the ripeness of that subtle pre-death season. Grace was absorbed by it, transfixed by the moving pictures of land-scape. The feeling she received from that countryside was somehow healing, even hopeful, and she had arrived in Wigton not only excited but sure that this was the real begin-ning of her new life, her motherhood.

The short walk from the bus stop next to Tickle's Lane, past the Victoria Arms and down Station Road to the big cobbled yard in which Mrs Johnston's house was situated drained some of the confidence of morning hope and the consolation of landscape out of her. Grace felt observed. She felt that her shame was on her like a placard hung around her neck.

Mrs Johnston, a stout, canny, efficient woman of experi-ence in these matters was brisk, believing that sentimentality would invite the sort of emotion she found it too difficult to cope with. Mrs Johnston, from a large country family, was steady, and steadiness was what she wanted from others.

She took Grace upstairs and left her beside Mary's cot. She stood beside her for a few moments, then went downstairs telling Grace to 'take as long as you like'. Mary was asleep, tiny hands flopped back beside her ears, breath like the lightest, slowest sigh over a still pond. Grace was reassured, just by her being. This baby had been part of her a few weeks ago. She felt the gap of her as she bent to breathe a kiss across her brow. Soon they would be together again. She could have scooped her up now and taken flight with her, but not this time. She had been told that sternly. Not this time. But how soon?

'Where would I take her is what they want to know,' she said to her father – at last able to talk openly and freely about this.

'You could come here with me.'

'You know I can't. There's no room as it is.'

'You and me together?' he said, rather wildly.

'We've been through that.'

There was the money. Those he was living with needed his contribution. Grace stilled the panic that threatened to ambush her these days. It was hard to hold out against a loss of control. The dream of living with her father and her daughter had been difficult to abandon.

'I want to know about my own mother,' she said. 'I want to know about her.'

'What can I tell you that I haven't already?'

'But that was when I was younger.'

He understood and lit up before he began. He looked tired, she thought: that bitten-in tiredness that comes from remorseless physical strain, that sense of a body all but worn out. He walked stiffly from the damage suffered in the pits. He had the appetite of a sparrow but still there was the flash of good looks about him that caught people's attention, and the smile that seemed to know the way the world worked and be amused at it.

'If I was to say one thing about her, it would be that she had courage,' he began. 'She took me on – a ragamuffin Irish papist. Everybody she knew told her I was the devil's spawn, as trusty as a bent penny. But once she had set her heart on me, she never wavered. She would have gone into the jaws of Hell and she very nearly did with your chapel elders! She said she would come over to the Catholic Church and she would have done. That was a big thing. But I went her way and it broke my mother's heart, so she told me, but . . .' he looked at Grace with a stab of implacable firmness '. . . I would have done anything in the world for your mother. Anything. I thought she had got herself a poor bargain, but she . . .' He paused.

He lit a new cigarette from the old stump. 'All I knew was country work and there wasn't much of that around, especially if you were outside the families and the cliques and most of all if you were Irish and even worse if you were a Catholic. Last to hire, first to fire. We lived on short commons. I had to go across the county at times just to get a couple of weeks' work. I would do any job they threw at me. I ate as little as they gave me and gave up drink – only these,' he waved the cigarette, 'I couldn't kick. But for the rest – it all went to her, what there was of it.'

'What else? What else about her courage?' That's what I want from her, Grace thought. That's how I want to be like her.

'Well. You see how Wilson and Sarah keep that farm. It's a handsome place. We lived in hovels. She can't have liked it but she never made me feel bad about it. She would always be cheering me up, telling me what a fine fellow I was.' He looked away and spoke very deliberately now. 'You can have no idea, Grace, and I hope you never will. There was a miscarriage before the first two and then we lost two more before Belle and yourself. But she wouldn't give in. And she could make something out of nothing. Whatever hovel we were in there would be something pleasant about it – a few flowers. Nothing got her down. She was alone more than was good when I was scavenging for work, and the scraping for the children you would have thought beneath a woman like her, but she never moaned.' He looked at Grace again, more tremulous now. 'You'll be thinking I'm talking of a saint, Grace, and I am. She was to me. I hope there's a next life just so's I'll have a chance to be with her again. There now. Nobody's ever got that out of me! There's a lot of her in you, Grace.' He took a sip of the tea and Grace let the wave of those last few words break slowly over her and lift her up and give her strength.

She went back to Grasmere by train and bus and felt that she had in her own hands a broken heart that, if she held it carefully enough, if she nursed it and above all if she had Ruth's courage, she could mend. She must not think of her life as ended. There was Mary.

Mrs Johnston was a kindly woman who had a good way with children, her own and those who went through her care. But she had her own rules and they were approved by the council. One rule was that too many visits would be upsetting for all parties and so Grace's visits were limited to one a month in the first year and then, she told Grace, there would be one every two months in the second and third year and, as the child might begin to get confused, visits would be stopped on any regular basis after the third year.

Grace had not expected any of that. Her view, misty but assured, was that within a few months a way would be found for them to be together. The consensus of those involved in making the decision was unequivocal. One or the other of them, mother or child, had to leave the area and if they wanted to stay together that was a matter for Grace alone to organise. It would have no help from the authorities and little sympathy from the population.

That was what she could not avoid. When she travelled north from the dale-bound secret shelter of genteel Grasmere, with its poetic associations and seasonal visits of gentle hill-walking ramblers, to the bleaker exposed flatlands of her home, she felt a coolness as sharp as a dramatic switch in the weather. An illegitimate child was to be feared and the reaction to that fear was rejection. It was not unlike having the plague and the woman was to be avoided. Even sympathy kept its voice low. She felt like an outcast on those journeys back to Oulton and that was not too great an exaggeration.

Alongside the mutual support in her old small community, alongside the chapel order and the insistence on manners, there was a darkness. There were wives in terror of drunken husbands; there were children beaten and strapped. A great sin was to let it be known. Without knowledge there was no judgement. With it came ancient and cruel punishment. An illegitimate child could become a focus of morality: to condemn it was to prove to each other how good they were.

Grace knew, and knew ever more strongly, that she was thought by many to be a fouled and lesser being. To let a child be brought up and nourished by such a one was resisted by all good people. Separation could be the only solution. The only godly solution.

There were times in the next months in Grasmere when Grace's body and spirit felt so heavy and weary that she hoped she might sleep never to wake. At times the pain became numb, which was the best she could wish for. But the merest cry of a child or reference to a birth would unnumb the pain for a few moments and bring back that agony of hope. Alan and Mary, both absent, both so deeply loved. It was too much to bear.

After almost a year of this, still unresolved, she decided to go and visit Alan's parents. She wrote them a letter and posted it two days before she set off. She would stay overnight and arrive in the morning. The letter would make it less of a shock for them but the time of its posting would close off the opportunity to repel her.

It had been growing inside her for months, this longing to join up again with Alan. She had tried very hard but finally it had broken through her defences. She had to make the connection, for all their sakes, she would tell herself, but most of all for her own. She could not just walk away and, besides, her love for him was unimpaired and who knew what a meeting might bring? Perhaps he was waiting for her . . .

CHAPTER NINETEEN

The five-thirty a.m. forecast said that the fine weather would hold over the north of England and it would be dry and with temperatures well above average for the time of year. John set off immediately. He made it in five hours, with five cigarettes, a pit stop just north of Birmingham and a drip feed from Radio 4. Along the way he phoned ahead to double check that his mother was having one of her good days and would not be fast asleep when he arrived. He kept the duty nurse informed of his progress. It became something of a game between them, and when he got there, he saluted. Beside her, Mary was in her wheelchair, and wrapped up as if the new ice age was prowling outside the door. She could not stand the cold and this would be her first time out of the home since the daffodil run.

Even the mild breeze from the sea alarmed her as he wheeled her across to the car.

'It's starvation,' she said. 'Oh dear! Where are we going?'

'Out,' he said, and he smiled at an instant memory of her asking when he was a boy, 'Where have you been?' 'Out,' was his complete answer. 'Out,' he repeated and, with the help of the nurse, heaved her into the front seat, put the wheelchair in the back of the car and waved goodbye.

'Bring her back safe!'

'See you,' said Mary and, entering into the spirit, she waved her hand in rather a royal manner.

'Goodbye, goodbye.' The car drew away. 'What was all that about?' she said.

He had planned an itinerary but the late-morning sun was so seductive he played with the notion of making a quick raid into the Lake District, which she had not visited for years. But it was a little too far, and it would be crowded on a Saturday like this, and . . .

He stuck to his plan but he took a winding way to Wigton so that she could enjoy some of the villages to which she had cycled on her morning delivery round for the post office in the years after the war. He said just enough to keep her company but saved his ammunition for the chief objective of the day, which was Wigton Revisited. She gazed out of the window intently, and now and then uttered praise, only praise, as if in the small allocation left of her life only praise was of value. The sun, the trees, a house, a garden, hedgerows, a few horses in a field, praise for them all. 'Look at . . .' 'Look at . . .' Never turning her head to him once, requiring no confirmation, absorbed in praising the passing present world.

John drove under the railway bridge, past the factory and into Station Road. He did not want to wear her out so he stoppered his tendency to recite the usual litany – that's the factory where Dad used to work, that's the sawmill where there was the big fire, that's the walk we used to take past the West Cumberland Farmers' buildings, that used to be Toppins farm, and Toppins field backed on to Mrs Johnston's house . . . and as Station Road rose into the town, he even managed to hold himself back from a eulogy on Redmayne's clothing factory in which Mary had worked from the age of fourteen to twenty-one, a factory that had dominated the road but had now disappeared without trace. A supermarket had taken over the territory. And Moore's garage and gift shop, the long-gone barber's shop, Billy Ivinson's stables, the Wallaces, the cake shop now a charity shop, the razed site of the grand Victoria Arms with a yard that could take three or four dozen shire horses on horse-fair days, all these were passed by. It was more than the triggering of a few sentences he hoped for this time.

He swung into what had been the yard where Mrs Johnston had lived and pulled up. Mary could see the house. He gave her time to settle herself, and then, 'It's changed a lot,' he said.

She did not respond but continued to gaze at the house. John was tentative.

'They've made it all one house. It's a big place now. They've painted it white ...' Compared with most of the houses in the town it had always been a big house. After her marriage, when her husband Harry had gone to war, she had returned. John had lived there until he was eight.

'They've laid a garden,' he said. 'It used to be a cobbled yard.'

'Look at the roses,' she said.

'It changes it a lot, doesn't it, being a garden?'

'We didn't have a garden,' she said. 'They're just a lot of work anyway.'

'And everything's gone except the house.'

'Where are we?'

'This is Station Road. This is Wigton.'

'Oh.' She was quiet. Were memories assembling, he wondered, moving into place across her mind, gradually putting together the scattered pieces of jigsaw from the past? This was the key location of her childhood, her adolescence, from this house she had been married; to this house she had returned for refuge in the war with her son, with him. Surely this would begin the great healing.

'There was such a lot in this yard,' he said. 'They called it the Council Yard. You wonder how it could have fitted in.'

Did she see herself as he saw her, a young woman hanging the sheets and shirts and other washing on one of the lines that were strung across the yard? There had been several lines, and other women in Station Road had used them on Mondays. John conjured up the washing day, the women moving between the sheets, pegs in their teeth, the mangle just outside the door and his mother letting him help her with it, squeezing out every drop of water they could. He saw her among the other women, he saw her sitting on the doorstep in the sun, he saw himself sitting on his first two-wheeler bicycle propped against the wall while he gathered his courage to let go. He saw his father coming back from the war and he knew he was misremembering how that had happened. But the force of it was still there, the footfalls, the entrances and the exits, the growing and the dying.

John remembered the dead body of Mrs Johnston. It was laid out in the barely used parlour and after a discussion he was allowed to see it. Did his mother take him through? She must have done. Clearly now, on this bright day, he saw the parlour gloom. Was there a candle? He remembered Mrs Johnston's face like wax and the urge to press his finger in that waxen cheek. In her lifetime he had been told to call her 'Grandma'.

'Did I live here?' she said.

'You *did*! You *did*!'

'It's very nice,' she said. And he waited . . .

'Sometimes I forget things, John. It's terrible.' She turned to him and smiled. 'But you'll remember, won't you?'

'Yes. Look. In that corner, up some steps, was the library.

Dad used to take me there on Fridays. It wasn't open every evening, just Tuesdays and Fridays, and then only for an hour or two. He used to talk to the librarian. I remember thinking that was really something. He could talk to anybody, though, couldn't he, Dad?' Damn!

'Your dad . . . Is he all right?'

'Yes.' How long? Fifteen years? 'Yes,' he repeated, and she looked away.

'Underneath the library was an estate agent's,' he continued hurriedly, 'Mr Dudding. He had pebble glasses and he wore his trilby hat even in the office. We could see him through the window.'

'Duddings . . . They were big church people, the Duddings.'

'Yes! And the fire station next to it! That was great, wasn't it?'

The factory hooter would wail across the town and the volunteer fire brigade would down tools and run or bike to the Council Yard to man the engine. By that time he could see a small crowd, mainly small children, gathering to cheer them on. He could not see his mother there.

'Upstairs, among the helmets and the uniforms and the spare hose, there were chairs and the silver band used it as a rehearsal room.'

'There was a horse,' she said. 'What was it called?'

'I can't remember.'

'You must remember. A horse, in a stable, on its own. Was it grey?'

'I think so.'

'You only think so?'

When she was a girl, did she go and feed the horse over the half-door of the stable? Very likely. Horses were there from the time she was a girl. There would have been two horses then for the old fire engine.

'And in that corner was where Mr Johnston kept his brushes and whatever for cleaning the streets.'

'He did. We got a reduction in rent for that. He was a nice man, Mr Johnston. Mrs Johnston was the boss. They were a very nice family, the Johnstons. And there were the black pipes' – she gestured to the left side of the garden, which ran into the back of a row of cottages – 'the council always kept pipes in our yard. I hated the pipes.'

'Mrs Johnston, you called her?'

'Mother. She was my mother.'

John saw Grace approaching the door to see her child and saw her again leaving alone. He saw the imprint of Grace's visits as clearly now as he saw his mother, the child, the girl, the young woman playing hide and seek with him among the damp, drying sheets. He longed to speak of Grace.

'She would take her chair out on a day like this,' she said, of Mrs Johnston. 'The boys would bring it out. And she would sit outside the house, just over there, when it was our house, and knit. They were always on the go, those women. They made everything.' Her look had become more concentrated, almost a stare.

'Just over there, she would sit just over there. I would get a cushion and sit at her feet and she would always have a job for you but she would talk to you. She looked after me . . . She was very kind, was Mrs Johnston . . .'

They stayed a little while longer. He took her to the church and would have taken her in – now and then she would say that she would like to go to church – but she showed no interest. Nor did anything else in the town stir her. He realised that he had hoped for a revelation and staved off disappointment . . . He would try again some other time.

He drove back to the coast and near the home he found a calm place to park. He had brought a flask of orange juice

186

and some shortbread. They sat and looked at the sea, the car windows open, hearing the calling of the gulls and in the distance muted music from the little fairground. She gazed out to the grey sea and was, he wanted to believe, content.

Another day.

CHAPTER TWENTY

It was the biggest journey Grace had ever made. On Carlisle Station she felt isolated even though there was a warm crowd and a prevalence of local accents. She felt a chill about her although the winter day was not especially cold. The traffic on the lines took most of her attention: the long, long goods trains, the men on the track checking the wheels with ringing hammers, the gushing of steam up to the vast dirty glass roof. Soot was already on her clothes. She was half an hour early.

She watched the soldiers closely as if she were trying to spot Alan even at this distance. They were very self-assured, she thought, unlike those she had known at Prospects. They stood in small groups; most of them smoked, and now and then there would be a small shout of common laughter. The war was over but the shock of peace had not yet been fully absorbed. The men could just as well have been setting off for the long haul to the Front. There would be no more fear of war for Alan now. That would help him, surely.

The grimy but, Grace thought, magnificent engine pulled in, drawing such a line of coaches that they stretched back to the bend in the track which swerved the traffic in from Scotland. There was no rush for seats. As yet the train was no more than half full. The whistles, the green flags, the more whistles, a *rat-a-tat* of slammed doors, the loud neighing from the engine and the train horse moved on.

Grace had secured a corner seat in one of the third-class compartments. It was dirty, but plush. Above the seats were sepia photographs of Morecambe Bay and Poole Harbour. The rack easily contained the small suitcase she had been loaned by Mrs Logan, the solicitor's wife. She had her sandwiches, which she would not eat on the train but in the room she had booked – with the help of a friend of Mr Logan – in a bed-and-breakfast hotel on the edge of Alan's small town. On her lap was the W. B. Yeats, which now she knew off by heart but was there as a refuge in case anyone threatened to intrude. She wanted to look out of the window at this new world as the train stopped and started through the landscape that undulated between familiar farmland and the grimy congestion of industry. She needed to steady her nerves all the way.

Grace wanted to wrap herself in her own thoughts and travel without contact but it proved impossible. A middle-aged couple took a shine to this young woman and plied her with questions and autobiography and food. Thankfully they left the train at Preston with a farewell that suggested a lasting friendship. The soldiers must have been in a separate section of the train because she neither saw nor heard them again after Carlisle. She realised that she would have been glad of their company, glad of a chance to talk about their experience of the war, glad to feel closer to Alan as the train took her closer to Birmingham and the excitement mixed with fearfulness.

What if he was so ill he could not see her or she was forbidden to see him? What if worse still had happened? What if his parents were angry with her for disobeying their request? At times, these and other questions welled up like tears, but she fought them off. She had to make this journey. It had become a pressure that would not be contained, a mission. She had to see Alan.

At Birmingham Grace went out of the industrial noise and surge of the station into the smog and manufacturing maelstrom of the 'Workshop of the World'. Birmingham, the claim was, could make anything you wanted. Grace walked for an hour or so, amazed at the complexity, the canals and the boat traffic, the hurrying of everyone, the glistening fog that at times seemed to make the workers appear caught in a ghostland they could not leave. She had been warned by the solicitor's wife that she would hate the city and its 'vulgarity', but Grace was enthralled by it. What a world was here! How did so many people fit in? Why were they all in such a hurry?

Nobody knew who she was! A prison door opened. Top hats and cloth caps on the same street, urchins like those she had read about in Charles Dickens. She realised that was partly why it was so unthreatening and so intriguing. She had read about it in his novels and other novels. Now she herself felt part of a novel, gliding through the soft smog, taking note of her route, which would thread her back to the station. Nobody knew who she was. Nobody cared and, for the first time in many months, she had a taste of freedom.

The bed-and-breakfast was a comfortable Victorian villa. Grace declined the offer of a snack but needed little persuasion to accept a cup of tea, which she took in the lounge where several guests were assembled in a whispering conference, waiting for bed.

She ate the sandwiches in her bedroom in a guilty manner, as if she were doing wrong and about to be told off. She was ravenous.

～

How could your step drag and float at the same time? Her throat was so dry. She felt empty even though she had made herself eat a creditable portion of the breakfast. She had left before nine and walked about the place for an hour, the high street cluttered with shops, the municipal park well inhabited by children on this Saturday morning. Grace had chosen Saturday because it was more likely that they would be in. They should have received her letter by now. Perhaps she had better go before Alan's mother went shopping. Perhaps she had gone earlier and Grace had passed her by on the street. Perhaps Alan had come back and would be there, with them, in the bungalow towards which she now walked with a steady step. The door knocker was the brass face of an elephant: you used the trunk to make the knock.

The door was half opened, and it must be Alfred; Grace knew it was Alfred. He had Alan's shape of face, the same mouth, something about the eyes. He looked at her without much interest. He was dressed, Grace thought, rather importantly. He wore a three-piece suit in brown tweed, a collar and a striped tie, which looked official. His brown brogues glittered.

It was she who had to begin.

'I'm Grace,' she said.

For a chasmic moment she thought that he simply did not recognise her name.

'Grace,' she repeated, with a feeling of sick humility.

His reaction was to frown.

'You'd better come in,' he said, and he glanced with some concern at the suitcase.

Alfred stood aside and let her precede him into the cramped hall.

'Elsie! We have a visitor.'

He waited until his wife appeared before speaking again.

'Grace,' he said, not in a friendly way, 'this is my wife, Mrs Marshall.'

'Grace?'

'Alan,' said Alfred. 'The letters.'

'Oh. Grace. Yes.'

'I suppose we had better go into the lounge,' said Alfred, and he led the way.

Grace put down her suitcase and decided against taking off her coat.

'I could make you a cup of tea.'

'No, thank you.'

Elsie's face expressed relief. Alan's hair, thought Grace, and the nose: certainly the reconstruction of Alan's face from the features of his parents was a useful, even a necessary distraction as she was ushered into the lounge. Alfred stood in front of the unlit fire and motioned to Grace and Elsie to take the armchairs that flanked it.

'This is very awkward,' he said. 'There's no getting away from the fact that this is very awkward.'

Elsie studied Grace closely while trying to pretend not to be doing so. She was impressed by the young woman's handsome looks, her self-possession, her apparent calm. And yet ... Grace, used to concealing turmoil, had set herself to be calm. It must be a shock for them. They had asked her not to intrude and here she was; clearly her letter had not yet arrived. It now seemed to her an unworthy manoeuvre, almost a deception.

'I wrote a letter,' she said, 'saying I would be coming here.'

'Lost in the post,' said Alfred, with no effort to conceal his disbelief. 'In any case, if I may say so, where we come from people wait to be invited. They don't just turn up out of the blue.'

'Alfred!'

'I speak my mind.'

'Are you sure you wouldn't like a cup of tea?'

'Yes, thank you.' She took a deep breath. 'I just wanted to see Alan, or at least to know how he was. I couldn't bear it any more, thinking of him so ill and not knowing. And . . .' Elsie looked alarmed and Grace went no further. She wanted to give her news to Alan first.

Elsie was trying desperately to communicate with Alfred by meaningful looks, which he ignored. It seemed to Grace, callow as she was in such matters, that Alfred was socially superior to Elsie and that she, conscious of his elevated position, was intimidated by him. Alfred levered himself on to his toes every now and then.

'Did you travel far?' Elsie asked of this young woman who had landed in their lounge as unexpectedly as a meteor.

'From Carlisle,' she said. 'I stayed overnight nearby.'

'With friends?'

'In a bed-and-breakfast hotel.'

'Oh dear,' said Elsie. 'Oh dear.'

It was Alfred's turn to resort to mime: his expression said, Don't you get too friendly.

Grace waited. The room was cold. It had the atmosphere of a room little lived-in. It was fanatically tidy. But, Grace noticed with pleasure, there was a fine glass-fronted bookcase. Alan would have read all of those. Elsie caught her glance. 'Alan was a big reader.' She smiled. 'It was difficult to tear him away from a book.'

Alfred began to charge a pipe, spinning out the process, concentrating on it.

'I know,' said Grace, released into an antechamber of happiness that she was talking with someone so close to Alan. 'Especially poetry.'

'He knew a lot of it by heart.' A proud mother. 'Sometimes when he said it I used to get goose pimples.'

Alfred jammed the tobacco down too hard. He used a match end to loosen it.

'Yes.' Grace smiled. 'He was so taken up with it he brought you into it as well.'

Elsie nodded, as if the explanation answered a long-unasked question.

Where is he now? thought Grace.

'Where is he now?' asked Grace, humbly.

The silence implied to Grace that something terrible had happened. She kept her nerve. Her fists tightened and her nails dug into her palms. She arched back against the chair.

'He was very bad,' said Elsie. 'Very bad. Wasn't he, Alfred?'

Her husband made a long stroke with the red matchhead and the rasp startled Grace. The flame was like a torch. He sucked hard at the pipe, his cheeks sunken, his eyes close-focused until the smoke finally convinced him that it was alight.

'He was given an honourable discharge.'

'It was nearly over anyway,' said Elsie.

'He was commended.'

The smoke billowed.

And now? Now?

'And now?'

'He's in Cornwall,' said Elsie, tentatively, 'almost his old self again.'

'Cornwall?'

'We used to go for holidays there, before the war. Alfred made friends with the bank manager.'

'He never talked to me about Cornwall.'

Why should he? said Alfred's expression.

195

'He kept himself very much to himself,' said Alfred, with approval.

'It's lovely down there,' said Elsie. 'Palm trees and the sea. I could look at the sea all day.'

'I expect they'll take their honeymoon down there,' said Alfred, looking firmly at Grace. 'Just along the coast from where they are now.' He put the pipe in his mouth and bit on it hard.

Grace felt that she had disappeared. Her body did not move, but that which was, consciously, her simply disappeared.

She woke to the gentle tapping of her face. She opened her eyes.

Elsie looked frightened. She had caught the truth in Grace and looked at the slightly thickened waist, not recovered from the birth, and she was terrified by what she sensed that she knew.

'Don't do that, Grace. Hello? Grace. Are you all right?'

'Yes,' she heard herself whisper the word. It came like a last breath.

'I'll get you that cup of tea.'

Elsie all but fled from the room. Alfred went across to the sideboard and brought back a silver-framed photograph and handed it to Grace. 'There you are,' he said. There was no obvious cruelty but he wanted, as he told Elsie later, 'to put an end to her nonsense once and for all'. 'On their engagement day.'

Grace studied the photograph. Alan looked so well, smiling, squinting rather at the sun, the sea behind him. His arm was round a young woman who seemed, to Grace, as happy as she could never be.

'Marion,' said Alfred. 'Daughter of our friends down there. They were childhood sweethearts.'

Grace examined the photograph with an expressionless intensity. This was the girl he had said was his sister. He had carried her photograph in his wallet.

'We always hoped it would happen,' he said, and took the silver frame out of her hands.

'Tea?' said Elsie.

'No, thank you.'

'Have a sip. It'll do you good. Just a sip.'

Disciplined to oblige, Grace took the cup and drank a little of the sweet tea. It helped. She paused, took another sip and handed back the cup. There was a terrible silence. How could she now tell them that they had a granddaughter? That Alan had a child? Out of the depths she heard herself say, 'One thing.' Both Alfred and Elsie froze to attention. 'I would . . . It would be better if Alan didn't know I'd been here.'

'I'm sure he'd like to know,' said Elsie, forcing the words through her choking throat.

'I think we should do as Grace requests,' said Alfred. He took out his pipe and held it in front of him, his hand poised there, like the minister, Grace thought, at the end of a service.

'I think we should respect what she says.' He rocked on his heels. 'And if I may say so, Grace, I respect you for saying it. Never fear, Alan will know nothing of this.'

Elsie subsided.

She insisted on walking Grace to the bus stop and Grace was glad of the company. And when the women parted, both of them knew the truth of it and Elsie, near tears, said, 'I'm so sorry, Grace.' And the young woman watched as the mother of Alan walked out of her life and did not look back.

Grace's mind found a way to wall in the shock and the hurt and the future. Walking slowly, like an old person, she arrived at the station and caught the first convenient train. The journey was a waking sleep. Her grief seemed so palpable that no one attempted to breach it. It was as though she were ill of an affliction that demanded isolation. When finally she arrived in Grasmere, in the dim lighting of the dark village, with the blackness of the hills about her, the silence of the village was a moment of balm. Perhaps she could just walk on, past the house, and go up the road towards the lake and hope for moonlight and walk along the shore. Perhaps she could never come back – just merge into the deep of the hills beside the lake and never be found.

CHAPTER TWENTY-ONE

Mary now lived mostly in the constant present. John would see his mother more frequently. Save exceptionally, there had been no past. There was no future. There was no point in referring to 'the last time I was here' or saying 'Next week we'll go out if the weather holds up.' Her past appeared to be an ocean of unknowing. Only now and then, prompted by John or by an unexpected breath of recognition, would cargo or wreckage from the past be washed on to the shore of the present. Her future was expressed in exclamations – 'That will be lovely!' 'I'd like that!' – that had no content. There were the occasions of recall, so rare, her last arias, John thought, her songs of remembrance.

He had finally come to the conclusion that she would never again be as she had been before. It was an obvious conclusion but it took him some time to accept it. He had known it for at least a year but there were different levels of knowing. It was only now that the intellectual sense of 'knowing' had turned into a visceral sense. Previously he knew it as an observable phenomenon but also as a problem that might be solved or alleviated – by new medicines, by time, by nursing, by his own amateur attempts to repair the ruin. Now he knew, as they used to say, 'in his bones' that she was relentlessly falling away from what she had been.

The most he could hope for her was a steady contentment as he watched her being transformed, like a butterfly slowly going back into its chrysalis.

The present was puzzling. One persistent mantra was that 'we only live in the present'. John thought that memory and planning challenged that mantra but here was a blunt truth of it. You were alive because of the breath you were taking now. However busy with the filing of recollections and the construction of future possibilities, that unique couple of handfuls of galactically sensitive stuff inside the eggshell skull was operating *now*. It only needed a now event – a heart attack, a bus, a bullet – and it would be all over. Back to particles, back into the cycles of billions of years to be part of the next act in the drama. But even then, John thought, it would still be now. Even if the particles did not realise that, though who knew what they thought? The present was forever there and its primacy was indisputable, however hedged in and jostled by what was gone and what was to come. It was the quick of life.

Yet when faced with this present, with his mother, John often found it hard to bear. He felt an intensity but there was also an inexcusable boredom. Maybe the present was just too hard. Maybe he could not face it. It was the clearest and most brutal reminder of death. Every breath you took was one less. Maybe the present was sliced up so minutely that only those who suffered from an affliction had the stamina to keep in it. Or perhaps it did not exist. When you thought of a word it was the future. When you spoke it, it was the past.

An alternative was to turn off the switch, let Mary be in her present world and leave him to rummage around the past and the future, only now and then lobbing back a polite and hopefully helpful remark. But that was a form of cheating, wasn't it? That was condescension. Not to try to be

200

engaged in her world was to leave her alone in it and how could he do that?

The other point was in John's too easy assumption that she was always much the same. The room would be spruce; family photographs on the wall, magazines, those fluffy toys brought by the grandchildren, a box of shortbread biscuits or chocolates on the side table. Mary would be asleep or in one of several recognisable degrees of wakefulness. The room was the same, with the view of trees and the dunes and a distant derelict industrial building that she was convinced had been a school. He could be lulled. Perhaps he wanted to be lulled. He wanted her to be anchored here, calm water lapping about her. But was not that a way to classify and dismiss her, to treat her as less than human?

The six-monthly phone calls from the psychiatrist disturbed these dreams of equilibrium, and the call he had taken earlier in the week had caused him to change his plans and, although she was in no danger, go to the home on the following Saturday.

There had been a 'marked deterioration' since his last visit, the psychiatrist reported. The pattern now seemed to be that she slept and stayed in her room for two days and then she would be lively enough to get up and join the others in the public rooms. On those days she could seem 'as right as rain'. But her food intake was increasingly variable. That could be made up with supplementary drinks. It was not a worry, the psychiatrist wrote. Her weight was 'pretty constant'. She showed no signs of the depression that could accompany dementia, which was a blessing. She did, however, have a growing tendency to be irritable and fractious with the nurses when they came to change her pads or wash her or move her. And she had started to spit out the pills – galantamine – that the nurses had a duty of care to make sure she took every morning. But they were very good with her, the psychiatrist said. They would leave her and come back in five or ten minutes when she would have forgotten all about the obstructive irritability and 'likely as not' she would be more placid a second time round. Just as Eileen, the nurse, had told him.

But it was a worry and he suggested she try a light course of citalopram. It took six to eight weeks to have an effect but it might calm her down. If it did not work then they would reconsider. He needed John's permission to deliver the drug.

John soon ran out of questions. The psychiatrist was so far ahead of him in knowledge of this drug that in the end John had to rely on him, which he did not find difficult. He had come to trust him. Rather self-consciously he gave his permission. So now there was a progression. There was a story leading to an ending.

~

He had been there since just before midday. She slept soundly, unmoving. He plugged in his laptop, put the mobile phone on silent but in view and settled down to the Middle Ages.

It was not a fashionable period for historical biography but John had been captured by it at university. His retirement had given him the chance to turn a part-time hobby into a full-time pursuit. He was working on John Wycliffe. Wycliffe was the man who had organised the first translation of the Bible into English. John felt a rare happiness as he sat there, invigilating the unconscious of his mother and excavating the conscience of this radical and erudite fourteenth-century Oxford theologian. If only they had not banned smoking and he had the nerve to ask for a cup of tea, life, in this small anteroom to nothingness, would have been near perfect.

But nothingness could not exist. That was one of the mysteries Wycliffe was exploring. Nothing could come of nothing. What that original and final something might be was the cause, the worth and the curse of religion. What was in Wycliffe's mind? That was the challenge John had set himself to take up. An astoundingly clever man he, like everyone else about him, believed that the Old Testament literally related the history of the world and the New Testament told the story of God's only begotten son coming to earth by way of a virgin in Bethlehem. He was a sensitive and radical man yet he had lived largely acceptingly in a society in which the Bible was used by the powerful to impose grotesque sexual domination by the male, slavery on the female, a time when the people tried to throw off serf-dom, a reign of terror on non-believers, and a time of a determination to exclude the majority from knowledge. But above all, as far as John was concerned, this great intellect unswervingly believed in eternal life. What could be learned from him on that subject?

What sort of mind did Wycliffe have? It was, John thought, much like the effort he made to understand what was happening in his mother's head. Only imagination could unlock it. Wycliffe, to his mother, to his own thoughts – how else could they be assembled out of the anarchy of sensations that bombarded them? But how had this conviction of the existence of a soul persisted through many thousands of years and been cleaved to by so many men and women in so many different civilisations?

~

The nurses came in at five to get her ready for the night and John went outside, to give them room and to devour the cigarette he had denied himself for almost three hours. What had they used for the addictive tendency in the Middle Ages? Beer and wine – there was plenty of that in the records. And a measure of complicated drugs – but nothing, surely, as stomach calming and mind sharpening as a cigarette.

When he returned, she was fully awake.

'Hello,' she said, with that lovely lilt of surprise and happiness, which made him feel that he had won a prize.

'It's been a long time,' she said.

'Yes.' He tidied away the laptop.

'I haven't seen your dad either.'

'No.'

'How is he?'

'He's well,' said John, making rather a business with the laptop.

'Is he?'

Her tone was sharp and he looked at her directly. 'Yes. He is.'

'Your dad we're talking about.'

'I know, yes. Harry.' He had been dead for fourteen years.

'Well? Is he all right?'

'Yes.'

She pointed her forefinger at him. He was convinced the lie was plain on his face.

'I'll believe you this time.'

'Good.'

There was a span of silence between them.

'I wish he would come and see me,' she said. 'I miss him terribly.'

He sat down beside her bed and took his mother's hand.

As usual it was cold. He massaged it lightly and said, 'Should I talk about Dad, about Harry?'

'Oh, yes! Oh, yes, please. Just to put me on. Till he can get here himself.'

'He would sit where I'm sitting,' said John, finding it difficult to keep his voice steady. He took a couple of deep breaths. 'He would have his left leg cocked over his right and be leaning forward, his elbow on his other knee, and in his other hand there would be a cigarette.'

'He liked his cigarettes.'

'He did. And then he would be doing what I'm doing. He would be holding your hand and trying to put some warmth into it. And he would talk away. He was a good talker.'

'He was! He was that.'

'He'd talk about who he bumped into up street that morning. There was Tommy Jackson.'

'He played the drums. He was a clever man, was Tommy. I was at school with his sister.'

'And Tommy told him he'd been offered a new job, in Shap, looking after a haunted house.'

'Tommy Jackson said that?'

'Yes. And then he met Francis Robinson with his pedigree Border terrier.'

'All those Robinson lads had dogs. Francis had a lovely voice. His mother was a friend of my mother.'

'He slipped into Martin's to put on a bet. Then across to the Kildare for a half. They talked about football and I'll tell you who was there, Arnold, Arnold Miller.'

'He was a lovely pianist.'

'He still is. And then he went to buy you some flowers – those white tulips over there that he asked me to bring for him because he knew I was visiting you. He said he would come and see you tomorrow.' He paused; her sweet and intense concentration was, suddenly, hard to bear.

'Then he went down to the allotments to talk to the pigeon men . . .' John said – and more . . .

And so, he hoped, Harry was in the room with her. He, too, saw his father as he told the story of his morning in the town. John saw the smile – 'He had a lovely smile,' his mother had once said, an unguarded, unexpected compliment. Then he saw a man shriven of petty faults, still ghosting around the town, missing his wife, looking for her.

He saw him now, more powerfully as the story went on. And he saw himself with his father. He was the child carried on his father's shoulders in the park, or being taken for a walk beside the river Wiza. Now his father was setting off to a dance with his mother, on their bicycles, both 'dressed up to the nines'. And while John spoke he looked at her and at the stillness of her, in a dream, he hoped, of his father whom she had met when she was sixteen and to whom she had been true and with whom she had kept faith ever since. And he talked more and more quietly until she fell asleep.

CHAPTER TWENTY-TWO

Work, for Grace, was the salvation. The Logan household had an inflexible routine. Morning: fires, breakfast, the beds, cleaning, shopping, and then what Grace was urged to call 'lunch'. Afternoon: tidying up, tea, or rather high tea, more like a supper at five, and a final snack at eight. Free time was not something sought. Free time was too available for thought, for regret, for pain. Activity could defer pain and pain deferred might weaken its hold. Every day when she woke up she had to steady herself. To get out of bed felt like levering herself out of a vault.

One part of the day struck calm and that was the morning's shopping. Mrs Logan liked the food to be fresh every day. She also liked Grace to be out of the house for a while. There was a heaviness in Grace's dutiful presence and a slight disturbance about her good looks (enhanced by Mrs Logan's knowledge of her sexual history) that made her absence necessary and welcome. Mrs Logan drew up her shopping list with care but also with some cunning so that Grace would have to criss-cross the village. And she would urge her 'not to rush' and insist that she need not be back before midday.

Grasmere was the perfect Lake District village. It carried a promise, in those post-war years, of healing through the presence of Nature. The guns of Passchendaele, Ypres and the Somme were finally silenced. The war memorial in the churchyard stood as a tribute to the past and a vow to the future that such a war would never happen again. The peacefulness of the landscape ringed the village and set it in that bowl, that vale, which had drawn in the Wordsworths and their friends. The small lake, the steep-climbing bare hills and the wooded paths, and all the harmony of form that had worked its way into the poetry of Wordsworth, and from him into the growing love of the landscape of a nation, was there for Grace to see and to sense.

Perhaps because it was so different from the bare uninter-rupted shallow seaward slope of the land on which she had grown up, these new prospects seemed so rich, so much more lively, so much more varied, pinching you with pleas-ure even when you were not looking for it. This was her one span of freedom from quiet desperation. She could not wait to step out of the door and be in the middle of it. She would look around her at the hills as if picking out friends, ancient, unchanging and unchangeable, in some direct but inexpli-cable way, a reassurance, above all a calming.

Early on in her employment Mrs Logan had caught her loitering by the grand, glass-fronted bookcases and told her she could take any book she wanted. She took down her own favourite – a fat, rather floridly bound selection of Wordsworth's poems, the shorter ones were the best, she said, and handed it over.

It was good for Grace to read these poems – of birds and flowers, of local places she was coming to know, of ordinary people in a tranquil area that, like the landscape on which they drew, began to help her lose that deadening numbness. She did not examine the reason for it but she found that her religion was little help to her. These poems became her hymn book now. They were blessedly at a distance from herself.

After a few months, Grace was looked out for in the village. She exuded an air of self-containment that impressed and pleased the residents of what had been until recently a remote and unvisited spot. She was like them. She knew about farming and village life. She kept herself to herself. She put on no airs even though she would have been entitled to a few, looking as she did. She was pleasant without overdoing it, and polite without making you feel put down. She became a favourite.

But there was another layer of life in the village, one that more intensely interested Grace. It was one that had built up since, and partly because of, the residence there of Dorothy and William Wordsworth and their family and friends. Followers of literary fashion began to take the trip to the Lake District. Painters, too, set up studios in Grasmere and elsewhere or came for a few weeks to produce a landscape for the London market. More recently, adventurous young men in boots and ropes had joined in with local climbers to go rock climbing. And there were ramblers sometimes from universities who came for walking holidays.

Grace liked to watch them. She liked to catch snatches of their conversation. She would sit on one of the two benches beside the stream or the seat outside the church and pretend to be reading or be absorbed in gazing around her, which was a common pursuit in the Lakes, and she would overhear sentences from these clusters of 'foreign' people, who sailed past her as confident as clouds. Their accents were different from those of Miss Birkett and the Logans, all of whom retained and rather relished a little local burr. Alan's accent had aimed for that of these ramblers. Perhaps she sat there and eavesdropped and played the innocent voyeur to innocent tourists in order to be able to think of Alan, a little, not have him dead inside her.

What world did these people live in? How amiable and relaxed they seemed. How full of laughter and earnest discussion. Sometimes they would sit nearby and she would be treated to a conversation that flitted from subject to subject like a butterfly flitting from flower to flower, so brightly, Grace thought, so attractively. Alan had been like that. She knew she could never be like that now. Books would be her equivalence and her consolation. But the sight – so many of them so handsomely sure of themselves – and the sound of them, could infuse her senses like the embracing landscape.

She worked for the Logans for nearly four years. Mrs Logan made two or three suggestions about 'an eligible local swain' but Grace's cool, stern reaction soon stopped that. Despite being integral to the functioning of their daily lives, Grace stood apart from them, which Mr Logan admired, Mrs Logan rather resented and Grace herself was not aware of.

She had her own path to walk. The ground lay between Mary and Ruth. Mary, she knew, as soon as she began to come out of that plunge of despair, had to be her prime concern. Ruth's courage, the knowledge of which was her father's gift to her, was her help and inspiration.

She went to see Mary at regular intervals during those years. Mrs Johnston's advice was reliable, she thought, and despite bouts of violent longing to take the child away, she resisted. Where could she keep her? Who would take both of them in?

Wilson was still alive, though now affected by a stroke that had put an end to all outside work. While he was in the house, Grace was not welcome, and that hurt her so much that she would not go to Oulton, not even to see Miss Birkett who, after the war had ended, had stayed in the Hall and remained there even after the death of her sister, though she still kept up Prospects. Grace corresponded with her and she was relieved that the older woman's advice complemented her own instinct. Now and then she would meet Sarah at Temple's tea rooms in Wigton on one of her visits to Mrs Johnston's. Grace was not comfortable in the town. She always felt stigmatised, the public sinner.

She went through to Wigton on Mary's fourth birthday. It was less conspicuous to buy the present in Keswick. She chose a doll in Victorian dress. A spare set of clothes went with it. There was a tiny umbrella. It was, by Mrs Johnston's standards, extravagant but not swanky. Grace wanted to spend money on her daughter. She sent the maintenance fee every week in the post with an extra sixpence for pocket money for her daughter. Mrs Johnston put the sixpences in a teapot for the future. Grace was thrifty. The plan was to amass as much as she could for the time when she and Mary could live together. That was the plan, the saving dream.

The little girl loved her birthday present. She hugged it and walked it and was soon murmuring to it. Grace had timed her visit for the early afternoon of a school day when Mrs Johnston would be alone in the house with Mary.

Grace could not take her eyes off the child. Mrs Johnston watched with a guarded tolerance. She liked this young woman even though she rather feared for a sudden switch of mood that would, she had told her husband, 'upset the apple cart'. But how could anyone not be moved by the hungry look, the struggle against tears, the thwarted passion?

Mary had the original clothes off the doll in a trice. The new set were admired and then a mixing of the clothes got under way, all the time the little girl cooing to the doll, cradling her and swaying with her, as Grace had so briefly done with the little girl herself.

'She's sharp enough,' said Mrs Johnston.

'Yes.'

'Still no trouble. And she talks away. She'll talk to that dolly for hours.'

'She looks very well,' said Grace, who knew that it would have been more accurate to say, 'She looks very happy,' but could not bring out those words.

'They all like her in the yard,' said Mrs Johnston. 'She's quite a favourite on washing day. She tries to help them to peg up the clothes. She can sing. She starts them off "The maid was in the garden hanging out the clothes,/When down came a blackbird and pecked off her nose."' Mrs Johnston laughed, a warm, tender laugh, Grace thought, a laugh that drew on a warm, tender memory, a mother's proud laugh. 'And some of them will pretend to peck off her nose.'

'It's a good yard for her to play in,' said Grace, dry-mouthed.

'And she likes the horse – she'll try to help with anything that's going and get under everybody's feet.'

'Look!' said Mary, and held out the doll to Grace.

'She's very pretty,' said Grace. Like you. Why could she not say 'like you'?

'Can I call her Sally?'

'Yes. I think Sally's just right. Sally. Where does Sally come from?'

Suddenly Grace was all but crushed with the voice of Alan reciting 'Down by the salley gardens, my love and I did meet . . .' She breathed in deeply.

'Sally Army,' said Mary.

'I take her to watch them play at the end of Water Street

at the end of a Saturday afternoon,' said Mrs Johnston, again proprietorially. 'She likes the big drum.'

'Sally's a good name.'

'Can I take her to bed with me?' Mary turned for permission to Mrs Johnston.

'You can, yes.'

'Can I take her upstairs now to see if she likes it?'

'Yes.'

Without a glance at Grace, the child went over to the stairs.

'She's a credit to you,' said Grace, with difficulty.

'She's your little girl,' said Mrs Johnston. 'I can see you in her every day.'

'Can you?'

'Oh, yes. There's no mistaking it.'

Grace nodded, rather brusquely, but gratefully . . .

Mary came back down. Grace had an all but mad longing to pick up the child and put her on her knee and hug her, hold her, smooth her hair, kiss her, be a mother and child. But it would confuse her, she thought, and she knew that Mrs Johnston thought the same.

When it was time to go, Mrs Johnston walked along the yard with her.

'I'm here while I'm needed,' she said.

'I know,' said Grace. 'Thank you.'

'If the time comes when your circumstances change, you only have to tell me and I'll pass her over.'

The two women stood together for a few moments and then, aware that their silent standing might draw attention to them in that crowded and inquisitive street, Grace said, 'I'll go now.'

'I feel for you,' Mrs Johnston said.

CHAPTER TWENTY-THREE

... Dr Fraser came to Prospects soon after you left [wrote Miss Birkett]. I found him most reliable and not at all difficult as were one or two of the other doctors. He married well and now practises in Carlisle, which would fit in with your plans. I have written to him. He will no doubt get in touch one way or the other. I have told him of your circumstances and I am certain he will be discreet.

Nothing much changes in Oulton which I find rather comforting. Whenever I see your grandmother she talks about you most affectionately.

Yours sincerely,
Margaret Birkett

Grace had waited almost six months for this. She had, unconsciously she realised, expected Miss Birkett to deliver an immediate response to her first letter. Her return note had seemed rather dry, concluding with the sentence 'I shall do my best for you but I do not want you to raise your hopes.' But now this! It had been worth the wait.

It was only later that Grace understood the care Miss Birkett had taken. Grace's decision to work in Carlisle had had the impact of a conversion. Carlisle was perfect! It was a big city where she would experience the anonymous freedom she had tasted in Birmingham. Oulton people rarely enough got to Wigton: the expense of the extra twelve miles to Carlisle was unthinkable for almost all of them. Carlisle was only half an hour on the bus from Wigton. The journey from Grasmere was lengthy and costly. She was already dreaming of possibilities and of Mary and herself united.

But for Miss Birkett it required the greatest discretion. She picked up the urgency of Grace's desire, but Miss Birkett would not let that influence her. It was no bad thing for Grace to be curbed. However much she sympathised – and she had taken the young woman to her heart – she saw a flaw that had not yet been eradicated: the recklessness, the lack of awareness of consequences. It would do her no harm to stay longer in Grasmere where, by all reports, she was doing well, even giving assistance to Mr Logan by copying out some of his documents in her fine handwriting.

Moreover, the right people were hard to find. They had to be broad-minded. What Grace had done was not publicly tolerated. In private there could be more flexibility but only a little. Such women were best sent far away from home. It followed, Miss Birkett reasoned, that absolute discretion was essential. There could be no gossip, none. They had to be a couple, a bachelor would not be acceptable. Finally there was the delicate matter, as Miss Birkett saw it, of tone. It would not do if Grace were to be overly pitied or condescended to. This was very difficult to guarantee. And the absence of the child would always be present in their minds. They had to be the sort of people who could override that, not scratch at it now and then, like a sore, or allude to it in moments of strain.

Miss Birkett was pleased that it had taken only six months. Everything had been explained to the Frasers. She had visited them in Carlisle and was satisfied. This, she thought, was the best destination Grace could hope for.

Matters moved slowly in Grasmere and Grace found that the cosiness of the place, its hemmed-in isolation, her unvarying routine, all that she had found protective, now seemed constraining. And although she found this a curious reflection, she had become too much part of it. In the winter and autumn it renewed its antique character as a small, slow Lakeland farming village and it was then that the few who lived there all the year round knitted closely together in secure communal warmth.

But Grace wanted away from it all. She wanted a life she could begin to shape for herself rather than one, however kindly, imposed on her.

Three months after she had received Miss Birkett's letter, she arrived in Carlisle. As soon as she stepped off the bus and into the crowded late-afternoon street, she relaxed. She asked directions and walked to her new home. The two bags were not heavy. She was a strong young woman.

~

Grace had two rooms to herself. They were attic rooms, sloping, gabled and plainly furnished. But there were two! An interconnecting door took her from the bedroom to what Mrs Fraser called her sitting room. 'This one was lying empty doing nothing,' she said, her cigarette used as a pointer, 'and so we thought we'd give you the use of it.' She looked around. 'It needs some pepping up but I expect we'll manage that, between us, as time goes on.' She took a puff at the cigarette and peered at the room. 'It's rather bare . . . Take your time to unpack and then come downstairs. I expect you'll be starving.'

Two rooms! She walked through the door from one to the other and then back. And then she did it again.

One for her and one for Mary. It was a sign.

In each of the rooms there was a window out of which, when she stood on the small stool, Grace saw a view she could look at and not tire of. The Frasers' large Victorian house was on a rise of land to the north of the city. The lower ground floor served as the surgery, which was entered by a side door. The ground floor held a sitting room, a kitchen and a dining room. On the first floor were two bedrooms and Dr Fraser's study. The boys' rooms were above that – 'the boys', Martin and Lionel, were fourteen and sixteen and 'away at school'. The attic rooms were up a twisting little staircase at the top, which, Grace was pleased to notice, gave the best view.

She looked down on the city, the medieval castle plumb in the foreground, the medieval cathedral and the big Victorian covered market just beyond, and beyond them the core of a city there in some form on that spot since the Romans had made it one of their strongest British fortresses. And, beyond the city, she saw a swathe of land speckled with farms and then the rise up to the northern fells, splendid in the distance, attracting their own weather of racing clouds and heavy rain.

Her nature, which she had steadied and which in the inner retreat of the Lakes had helped heal itself, now began to feel something of its old confidence.

She sat on the bed and looked at her estate. She was deeply pleased. The sensation went through a mind unaccustomed to such material pleasure. She smiled to herself and tried to bounce up and down on the ironing board of a bed. She would buy a softer mattress for Mary.

But – careful! she counselled herself. Careful. One step

at a time. Inch by inch. She had let the genie of exhilaration out of the bottle. It had to be put back in, firmly, and the bottle stoppered. She had not schooled herself to outward patience for those years to throw it away now. One step at a time.

She went down the twisting stairs. Halfway down was a bathroom. Presumably she could use that one. Perhaps it was for her sole use. She would ask. It was odd how awkward she felt in anticipation of asking such a simple question.

The Frasers were a busy couple. He took on more than his share of non-paying patients. He was also active in the town: on the committee of the rugby club, a golfer, and a Rotarian. George Fraser, who had played in the pack of the Carlisle rugby team in his day, was as burly as you could wish for in a comforting doctor. He wore one of his three heavy three-piece tweed suits for most of the year and was pleased to point out their great age. His ruddy face was well weathered and well whiskied. He rather cultivated the padding gait of a bear.

Agnes was stringy, more intense than her husband but not oppressively so. Her thick, corn-coloured hair was scraped into what looked like a rather painful severity. She wore the merest dab of makeup. Her nose was strong and dominated a slim face, stern but easily provoked to laughter. Her time, since 'the boys' had gone, was partly devoted to running a small infants school in a nearby slum, a free school that she had founded. Her other passion, not entirely appropriate, it was thought, for a doctor's wife, was politics. She had been a suffragette.

'I think she'll do very well,' she said, a few evenings later. They always talked through the day over his last whisky. Agnes rarely drank.

'C and P,' said her husband. 'Character and potential.'

'There isn't such a terrible lot to do, in fact. With the boys gone the place is quite presentable. She goes through it like a knife through butter.'

'Efficient?'

'Ten out of ten. You're always droning on about your filing and the other stuff. I'm sure she could help you with that. It would give her more of an interest.'

'She'll need to type.'

'Even you can type.'

'One finger.'

'I'm sure she'll be equal to it. It's not exactly a high standard you set.'

Grace's interests were building up. But in the first months it was her keenest pleasure to walk in the centre of the city and especially in the covered market. There were times when she was hemmed in by people, all but jostled by the shoppers, trying to pick out the calls of the stallholders, crushed but serene that she was there, with all the others, just one of a crowd. The immersion into others was a baptism into her new life.

And there were Mrs Fraser's books – detective stories, many of them, freely urged on Grace whom she had 'spotted as a reader' and, uniquely in Grace's experience, happy to talk about them with her. 'George reads nothing but the *Carlisle Journal*,' she said. She would lend Grace books by Dorothy L. Sayers and Conan Doyle and Agatha Christie and others and seek out her opinion on them. Nor did she allow just a tokenistic 'I liked it' or 'Not as good as the others.' Agnes enjoyed talking about the characters – were they believable? That was the crucial thing, she said. If you didn't believe in a character how could you possibly go on? And did the writers cheat with the plots? Grace began to go to the library. And so, gently, Grace was led into talk about politics and ideas of the day, which gave her both confidence and another interest.

Over that first year, there were regular visits to Wigton, but she held her fire. There was the weekly letter enclosing the maintenance and the weekly reply of two or three lines. Thank you for the money. Mary is well.

The two attic rooms had assumed some of the glow of Sarah's kitchen. Agnes had shuttled up from the cellars a few pieces of brown furniture, which responded to high polish. She had also found a couple of rugs in there and two prints of the Scottish Highlands. Grace had broken her vow of thrift to buy a second-hand flower vase, a jug, a candle-holder, two china shepherdesses in frilly dresses, which Mary would surely like, and a few other knick-knacks from the quaint poky little shops in the lanes in the middle of the city. And books: there was the beginning of a library. She felt fortunate. Soon she would be reunited with Mary. Her heart was lighter, her step had a spring in it: life would be good.

CHAPTER TWENTY-FOUR

'I remember that cupboard,' John said. 'It was to the left-hand side of the fireplace in the kitchen. Grandma Johnston kept "rummage" in it. "Go and have a rummage," that's what she would say.'

'That's what she said to me as well!' said Mary, well enough to sit in the chair beside her bed, cushioned and upright.

'There was a brass box beside it. It was decorated with a picture of a village street, two men walking in different directions and two dogs, I think, and thatched cottages – all done in brass. You still have it,' he said.

'Do I?'

'In your house.'

'That's good.' She pointed her forefinger. 'You have a good memory. That's very good. In my house.'

The furniture was in store. The few articles of sentimental value had been taken to London for safe keeping. The brass box was now in John's study.

John's father Harry had joined up for the Second War. Mary had moved from the house in the yard with the wash-house and lavatory she shared with three other families and gone back to 'Mother's'. John had lived there throughout the war and for a few years after it when his father had come back and they had been unable to get suitable accommodation. At times it seemed that his mother's years in that unchanging house and that unchanging yard and his own time there were one and the same life. By the time John arrived there Mother Johnston was a stout matriarch, her boys now men; the other foster-child had moved south and there were two lodgers and yet . . . John's recollections included a slow ease of daily life as well as sudden pitches of anger, a secure sense of refuge in that little higgledy-piggledy community.

'I would sometimes hide in that cupboard when I thought she wanted me to do a job,' Mary said. 'Mind you, she knew where I was. She just pretended she didn't. And sometimes when Grace came.'

'So *you* hid in the cupboard as well,' he said, bringing her back, he hoped, to where they had begun. It was a good day, one of her better days. The energy for it seemed to be in this memory of fear. 'Why was that?'

'I thought she wanted to take me from my mother.'

He waited for her to go on. He wanted her to say that the woman who wanted to take her away was her own mother. But he was too afraid it would upset her.

'I wanted to stay with Mother. I didn't want to be taken away,' she said. 'The Johnstons were a very nice family.'

~

Grace had worked it out and put her plan on paper. This made it seem more real. She liked settling at the table in her sitting room, a small coal fire, the curtains always open, an armchair, a rug, the prints, with luck a few flowers from the garden in the vase she had bought. It was as if the room extended her, added to her, and yet protected her. It seemed so intimately hers and hers alone. No one else ever entered. A small bell outside the door would summon her from time to time but she knew her hours. And this writing pad was another extension to her mind.

She had begun to do some secretarial work for Dr Fraser and the novelty of it had engaged her interest immediately. Soon she became involved with the lives of those whose files she catalogued. He encouraged her to help him. He had taught her how to put the instruments in carbolic acid. He liked to spend a few minutes with her after morning surgery going through his diary. Already she could type as quickly and more neatly than he. But she preferred to handwrite. It seemed more authoritative. Agnes complimented her on her hand. Grace immediately ascribed it to the teaching of Miss Errington, who had taught them all the copperplate script.

Now that she was settled in the city and in her work, to sit alone in the evening with book and pen, in her sacred sitting room perched on top of a house on a hill, was better far than anything else. In that solitude she could find her own company. She could 'suffer her own company well', as people in her childhood had phrased it. And the pen took her out of that self. A few strokes, a few words, and the lists – there were many lists – would grow, and from the lists possible worlds would flow. She kept an occasional record – it had not the daily rigour of a diary – of observation and opinion on what she saw and heard. These were locked away in the only drawer in the two rooms that had a key and the key was buried at the bottom of her pocket. Sometimes she would even write a few paragraphs about the village she had come from, which now seemed marooned in her past, neither dead nor alive.

But the lists that were the longest were the lists about Mary. One of them was devoted to places she could take her away to for day trips, perhaps even for a weekend. That would be the best way to start, she thought. After that, after several outings, she would approach Dr Fraser about bringing the child to live with her – a child old enough by then not to be a nuisance. Finally she would talk to Mrs Johnston and to Mary herself.

One thing at a time.

She took the bus to Wigton. She was more comfortable in the town now. Or stronger? She walked around to the house in the Council Yard on a summer's afternoon, still cautious but without the burn of shame.

The women sat outside the house in the warmth of the sun and Mrs Johnston brought out tea. Mary had said a polite hello, held out the ageing doll as evidence of continuing gratitude, and slipped back inside the house when the women began to talk of matters that bored the little girl.

But her ears were pricked up. She had sensed they might be talking about her. She was never far from the open door. Her mother and the other woman would often talk about her and she did not want to miss that. She was puzzled by Grace, as she had been instructed to call her. She seemed too old to call by her first name. She was very kind and Mary knew that Grace liked her but she did not know why Grace was there, and so regularly, and yet when she arrived Mrs Johnston made special efforts and she herself had to look presentable. Then there would be the presents – always something, a sixpence, a packet of sweets . . . The girl kept a literal distance from her, as if she feared being snatched away. And this fear fed into what she now overheard.

'I thought I'd take her away next month,' said Grace. 'At the beginning of the summer holidays.'

'That would be a good time,' Mary heard Mother Johnston reply.

'Do you think she would mind?'

'You'd have to ask her but she's biddable. She'll do as I say.'

'And what will you say?' Mary caught the anxiety, which fed her own rising panic.

'I'll tell her she must go with you.'

Mary fled to hide in the cupboard.

~

'I hid in that cupboard,' she said again.

'It was roomy.'

'They both came into the house to look for me.' Mary's remembered distress began to seep into her expression.

'But they didn't find you,' said John. 'They didn't know where you were.'

'Mother Johnston would have known.'

John left it at that.

~

Mrs Johnston had pointed to the cupboard and smiled and whispered, 'Little piggies have big ears.' Then she cooed, 'Mary! Mar-ee, where are you? Grace wants to talk to you. Where are you?' The older woman smiled again at Grace, whose responding smile was strained. This was a game between Mrs Johnston and Mary, between the mother and her child, a game deeply planted in simple but loved hide-and-seek games in the child's past, her child's past, a game that was layered with experiences she would never have.

A terrible jealousy took hold of Grace, and all her lists

227

and loving plans were thrown on to the bonfire of this possession by jealousy.

'Leave her,' she said. 'I'll come back another time.'

'She's a lovely little girl,' said Mrs Johnston, smiling.

Grace walked out rapidly, not wishing to be impeded, not wishing to be calmed down, not wanting to be there.

~

It was like a firestorm. It raged through her, destroying her peace of mind, racking her sleep, impairing her work. Dr Fraser found no ailment but he recognised distress when he saw it. He prescribed strong sedatives and a few days' rest. Grace resisted them. The routine was what held her together. Work worked, she knew that.

She remembered spasms of grief over the mother she had never known. This was even more fierce. The childhood of her daughter from which she had been banned. What sort of religion condoned and enforced that? What Immortal Invisible God Only Wise allowed that? And turned an apparently amiable village community into a hunting pack, after her blood, taking a sort of revenge on her for unpermitted pleasure, vengeance for a passion, condemnation for an accident.

Grace admitted to herself that she hated religion. She had gone to the Anglican church in Grasmere but only because not to have gone would have drawn to her the sort of attention she sought to avoid. So she went for that service of social solicitude, Evensong. Work could excuse her attendance at the Eucharist in the morning, when in any case the constant standing and sitting and kneeling, the creeds, the versicles and responses and the barbaric declaration that the congregation was about to eat the body and drink the blood of Jesus Christ offended her Spartan nonconformist inheritance. She had to cook the Sunday meal, to which Mr Logan always invited guests. She had adopted a similar tactic in Carlisle, although the minimally dutiful Dr Fraser and the clearly tokenistic visits of Agnes gave her a much looser rein.

So where did you turn if you had no God? She read from the Wordsworth selection Mrs Logan had given her. She found little there for the salving of the jealousy that had seized her. She walked, whenever she could, through the city and into the park, which reached into the countryside. She walked on the bank of the river Eden with no other purpose than to tire herself out.

The Frasers did not question her but they were well aware of the root of the unhappiness. They waited a while until Agnes said, 'It's gone on long enough. I'll talk to her after lunch. You'll be playing golf.'

Agnes suggested they go into the drawing room and Grace feared the worst. She knew her work had been less than satisfactory. She had caught the glances between them. She looked a sight. She was perpetually tired. She had a small but persistent and irritating scratchy cough. She needed this job.

'I'm not going to pry, Grace. I can understand that might just make it worse. Some matters have to be seen through by ourselves alone. I fear you've had rather too much experience of that. Of course, if you chose to . . .'

Grace sat before her like a criminal, waiting for the sentence.

'Would you like to work with me at the school?' said Agnes. 'I need help with the very little ones, the threes and fours. Some of them have a tough time on the home front.

They need more attention than Mrs Dawson or myself can give them. I've talked to Dr Fraser. We think we can reorganise your work so that you can be at the school two or three afternoons a week from about one o'clock until three. Does it interest you? I'm sure you're quite capable of doing it.'

Sometimes there are acts of pure kindness that can change a life. This offer was to be one of those. Grace reined in her feelings and was outwardly calm but teaching those often under-nourished, under-loved children was to be like receiving a sacrament. She was, at last, able to be with, to watch over, to help and love children; and slowly the weight of grief in her was anaesthetised and replaced, to some extent at least, by the knowledge that she was wanted and that she could give what her life so far had barred her from giving.

~

Almost a year later, there was a brief note from Mrs Johnston. Could Grace come as soon as possible? Preferably on a Saturday.

Mrs Johnston immediately led her into the parlour, so little used that it had the atmosphere of being in constant mourning. There was an unplayed piano, a rarely sat-on three-piece suite, a polished fireplace emitting warmth no more than two or three times a year, and the smell of dust from the heavy carpets despite weekly beating. There had been no sight of Mary. Grace was still prey to so many fears that she lowered her top lip and pressed her teeth into it.

Mrs Johnston took one armchair, Grace the other.

'I have to tell you this,' said Mrs Johnston. 'I think you are the only one who can do what is needful.'

Grace had to keep quiet. Was that the goal of all her effort? To wait?

'She came back from school the day I wrote you that letter. She was in a state. I'll not drag it out. Somebody in the schoolyard, some girl, they have separate yards, the boys and the girls, some girl had told her that she was . . . a bastard.'

Grace put her hand to her mouth to stop herself crying out. Her head leaned back as if reacting against a blow. She tried to swallow but her throat was too constricted. She waited.

'She wouldn't say who it was but if I find out . . . It seems that others joined in. When the bell went for school over, two of them followed her down the high street shouting out, "Mary is a bastard!"' Mrs Johnston paused. Her anger was undiminished. 'Poor little lass,' she said. 'Now then . . . Now . . . She wants to know what it means. She's nearly eight now and she's sharp. She can understand things. She wants to know what it means and you have to tell her. You have to tell her today. I'm going round to see her teacher later on this afternoon. There we are, Grace. She's upstairs. I've said you're taking her for a walk.'

Grace took her across Market Hill, along the Tenters, and at the bottom of Stony Hill she turned left on to the path that led through several fields to the hamlet of Kirkland. It was a calm walk: open fields were on both sides of the path; there was a picturesque copse of Scots pines in the pasture land belonging to the big house, fat cattle grazed, scarcely moving, the small soothing sounds of a sweet summer day.

'We could sit here,' said Grace. There was a small section left of the stone wall that had tumbled down.

Mary, who had been very quiet, aware that something important was going to happen, sat down obediently and clutched her doll tightly.

Grace had to do it.

'Mrs Johnston . . .' said Grace.

'Mother . . .' said Mary, quickly, and Grace knew that was not her.

'Yes. She told me that somebody . . .'

'I'm not telling . . .'

'That's not . . . that's fine. That somebody had said you were a bastard.'

Mary was so very still and silent that Grace felt it like a force.

'And they meant to be nasty,' said Grace.

'They were!' Mary looked away.

'A bastard means . . . it means that . . .' It means that I should not lie. It means that this is my legacy to my daughter. It means that I have to do it.

'It means that people think you have no daddy and just a mammy.'

Grace thought that Mary's stillness, if it were possible, intensified.

'Well, that's not true, Mary. You have a mammy. It's a difficult, it's not an easy story, but I am your mammy.'

'No, you're not!'

Still the girl did not turn to look at her.

'And you have a daddy.'

'Well, where is he?'

This was almost too much for Grace. For both of them. But Grace knew that she had to go through with it.

'He went away. He was a soldier in the war. He was very brave but he was wounded. And then he went away. And I didn't see him again.'

'Why?'

Oh, yes, why? . . . Why?

'It was the war. Terrible things happened in the war.'

232

'Where is he now?'

'I don't know, Mary. I don't know.'

And now Grace looked away over the field at the tall pines, wishing that her life and Mary's life could have been different – as simple, as aching and as impossible a wish as that.

The child did not speak. Grace had to do it.

'So. It isn't true, you see. What they said is not true. You are not . . . that word.'

And where would the lie later fall?

Mary stood up, so troubled, Grace thought, so unfairly troubled. The girl searched into Grace's expression. Grace held her gaze. She stood up and they waited in silence for a moment, and then Mary held out her hand and they walked back into the town.

CHAPTER TWENTY-FIVE

Perhaps some things were better left unsaid, Grace thought, as she looked out of the bus window at the familiar landscape. How strong was Mary? Would this knowledge help her or make her more bewildered? Grace was uneasy. Mary had taken her hand and they had walked close together, treading lightly, Grace thought, thin ice. A new path? But as soon as they had reached the house, Mary had let go and, in a rush, gone to Mrs Johnston and clung to her, hiding her face in the broad apron: she made no sound but dug her head in deep. Mrs Johnston looked satisfied and stroked the little girl's hair. Grace thought that it was she who should have done that. Why hadn't she? She felt breathless and it was with difficulty that she said, 'We talked about it. I told her that she did have a mammy and a daddy.'

She paused. She said, 'I told her I was her mammy, and her daddy had gone away after the war. That he was a brave soldier.'

Again she paused. Knowing that her words were addressed to the child.

'I should have said more. I should have said that you were looking after her now and for a while. I should have said that you were being her mother now while I . . .'

'You'd not been well,' said Mrs Johnston, uninterruptedly stroking the child's head.

'That's true. I've not been well.'

'And you come whenever you can.'

'Yes.'

'And we'll see what happens.'

'We will,' said Grace. 'I think I'll go now . . . Mary?'

The child released herself and looked at Grace and then at Mrs Johnston. It was a very serious look, she gave, her eyes unstained by tears.

'I'll see you again soon,' said Grace.

Mary nodded and pressed the doll to her chest.

'There you are, then,' said Mrs Johnston. 'It'll all get over.'

But she kept a close eye on the girl. Mrs Johnston believed that you had to meet your troubles head on. Certain matters were private, certain information was rightly secret. But once the devil surfaced you had to fight him and destroy him or he would never go away. It was years since she had attended a chapel service – she was a Congregationalist – but the basic notion that the world was divided between the good and the bad, that the devil would get you unless you were on your guard and that when you saw him at work you had to fight him off, was rooted in her. Little girls calling Mary a 'bastard' was the work of the devil. He had to be faced down and the strongest weapon was truth. And if not truth . . . ?

There was close observation. Mrs Johnston watched over Mary in the subsequent weeks and she was not reassured. It had set her back. Previously, on most mornings, soon after Mary woke up, she would start singing. Mrs Johnston thought it was the loveliest sound there was, the sweet little bird voice piping the old schoolroom songs that she, too, had learned and in the same schoolroom years before. It

236

gave the house a blessing, she thought, it heralded the day, that sweet voice; it was her own dawn.

Now there was silence. Mrs Johnston felt helpless and nervous at the morning silence. At first she poked her head into the cubbyhole of a room in which the girl slept. She would be awake, quietly playing with the doll or looking through one of the children's books Grace had bought her. She would offer up a smile and Mrs Johnston would say, over-roughly, 'It's time you were up and about,' and the girl would get out of her bed instantly, take off her nightgown and begin to dress for the day.

'Have they stopped calling you that word?' she asked, a few weeks on.

'Yes,' Mary replied shortly.

The schoolteacher had been distressed at Mrs Johnston's report and promised that she would 'stamp it out', which she had done. But for Mary it hung around in the playground, like a placard around her neck. It never quite went away; even the years to come did not totally dispel it. For Mary that playground had lost the perfection it had once held, as a place of unique happiness, the girls, her friends, singing skipping songs, playing hopscotch in the chalked squares, running around in giddy games of tiggy in the flagged yard, a never failing pleasure mid-morning, mid-afternoon. Now she walked out circumspectly at break times, a film of fear about her but steeling herself not to show it.

Her marks in the class, which had been high, dwindled to the middle range. The teacher was disappointed. She had hoped Mary might surprise them all. But she resisted coaxing. She had 'gone into herself', Mrs Johnston wrote to Grace, and she wondered if she had done the right thing. 'I blame myself,' Mrs Johnston wrote, and added, 'Maybe some things are best left alone.'

As the bruises came out, bruises from the blow of the word and the revelations from her new mother, Mary was to find that many questions were let loose that troubled her and could not be answered. These continued over the years and over much of her life. An intense interiority began, a sadness that she disguised with skill and fought unremittingly because sadness made you conspicuous and people asked you questions about it and she had so much to be thankful for. But they were there now and they would never go away, the questions: why had she not been with her real mother all the time? Why did her real mother not go and find her father? Why did she want another mother when she had Mrs Johnston? She looked around at her playmates: was she the only one?

She had to watch out for herself now.

And yet ... the growing older, the shucking off of old skins, the intimacies in the small town, the early and later the uncompromised and unbroken 'love' (a word she always stumbled on) for her boyfriend, her fiancé, her husband, Harry, clever, funny Harry, from a big family that absorbed her, the arrival of John, her own child ... At some stage she escaped and put it behind her, somehow in the strange complexity of life both forgetting and remembering it, now a pressure, now a shadow, now no more than a faint scent.

A few months on after that meeting with Grace, Mrs Johnston stopped work in the early-morning kitchen and looked to the ceiling and felt a deep release of relief as Mary sang, 'Polly put the kettle on, Polly put the kettle on, Polly put the kettle on, We'll all have tea.'

~

Grace knew that she had lost but she would not yet give in. She spoke to Agnes.

'What she wants is quite impossible,' said Agnes, later, to her husband.

'Let's take a little time to talk about it.' He was not keen on the last whisky of the day being accompanied by gunfire.

Agnes all but bit on the cigarette as she took a quick puff.

'She's become very valuable to us,' George continued. 'And we are both very fond of her.' He pinged the crystal whisky tumbler with the nail of his forefinger. 'Number one' – ping! – 'the house is spick and span, the meals are on the table when they should be. Second point' – ping! – 'she's sorted out my office – with help from me, I admit, but only at the start. She soon got the hang of it. I'm better organised than I've ever been.' Ping! 'Last, but not least, you tell me she's a Trojan at the school.'

'All true,' said Agnes. 'But,' another deep pull on the cigarette, 'I do not think it would work were we to have a small child in this house day and night. We've done that. Grace couldn't help being distracted. We can both guess how much she would dote on the child – and she would want her friends to come here – and why not? – and the interminable illnesses . . . I feel bad about it but I also refuse to feel bad about it. We didn't agree to that.'

'It means a lot to her.'

'I know. I know! Don't make me feel like the wicked witch. She is very good with the children. She has the knack of teaching them to read, even the urchins. She reads them stories and makes up stories for them about life on a farm. They draw cows and pigs and horses. How much more will she be devoted to her own daughter? And when the boys come home. And when they start to bring their friends – it's all too complicated and I am sorry, George, but I don't want

it to be complicated. I'm selfish, I know, and unchar-
itable . . .'

'No, no . . . you've reasoned it through, that's all.'

He allowed himself a second dash of the Bell's. 'So how
will you tell her?'

'I hoped you would do that,' said Agnes. 'I'm no good at
tact.'

'It would be a great shame to lose her.'

'I'm sorry. But I refuse to carry all that guilt. It's too much
to ask of me.'

~

Grace next went to Wigton two weeks after she had followed
Mrs Johnston's request to explain away the 'bastard'. She,
too, was uneasy about having done it. The flurry of the
moment and Mrs Johnston's characteristic implacability
had given her no space for reflection. But what option was
there? The dream of the perfect moment when she would
reveal herself to her daughter had never been more than a
dream. And surely the word and the wound of 'bastard' had
to be addressed and the sooner the better. And she was the
one who had to do it even if, in the process, she was now
convinced, it had driven a wedge between them. She feared
that Mary would never trust her now.

Add to that the crushingly kindly manner in which Dr
Fraser (speaking, Grace knew, for his wife) had rejected her
tentative suggestion, and she felt a vertigo in her soul. She
realised that now she had no rudder, no steer. She had her
will, that was all, and that will could be strengthened and it
could and it would see her through, she knew that. To give
up her dream would bring least harm. That was her

decision, her conclusion. That was what she would bend herself to ...

When she arrived in Wigton, instead of going to the house she returned to the broken wall on the path to Kirkland where she had tried to dispel Mary's fear. She was self-conscious about this. It seemed too 'dramatic', she thought, and too public, although who on earth would comment on a woman taking a few minutes' rest on a country walk? But the turbulence she had to subdue had returned in full spate: she needed ... space? Solitude? Both, and the courage of her mother. She sat there for a while and hoped for steadiness. There would be many times like this.

Then, briskly, she went to see Mary. She had bought her a book of line drawings of farm animals and some coloured pencils.

The girl was unaffectedly pleased to see her and the book and especially the coloured pencils, which she received like gifts from the gods. She began to fill in the animals immediately. The women watched her, some sort of harmony between them.

'I always wanted a girl,' said Mrs Johnston.

~

Perhaps the insistence on prayer in the chapel and its regular repetition throughout her childhood had given to Grace an ability to concentrate intensely, which she would otherwise not have had. Now, although she had deserted her religion, this gift remained. In her attic room, on the Sunday afternoon, the south-facing windows ablaze with sun, she sat and thought it all through. It required a discipline of devotion, but she called that up. Echoes of all the old chapel certainties whispered around the aisles of her mind. The world of the chapel was a simple place and the prize went to the righteous. She was no longer of that company. But she could find strength in what she had been taught.

Grace had, by now, experience of being failed by life and returning to it; of being self-exiled and enduring it and returning to the fray; of being rejected by love and coming out of the despair; of finding a purpose in life, and then being denied the chance to carry it through.

She would have to build a life of her own and on her own. It was a life not chosen but chosen for her, as it was for many others. She would plant the life in what she had and hope no more. She would not cry. But nor would she give in. A distant amen came to seal her resolution. So be it.

CHAPTER TWENTY-SIX

Grace kept her attic view and Mary kept her distance. Once, Mary told John, they passed each other on the street when Mary was fourteen and about to leave school and work in the local factory. The encounter was in King Street. Mary was going up the street to shop, Grace coming down the street for the bus. They were on the same pavement. Each saw the other with about fifty yards between them. A drab street, that northern winter afternoon. Drab and sad with the workless men propping up the walls and the feeling of listlessness in a town that seemed to be dying by the day in the deep post-war depression.

Between the two there was a glance of light. Yet still, still it stayed, the paralysing stigma. Grace moved towards the shop frontage, Mary to the outer edge, to the pavement's kerb, so that they would not meet. John remembered Mary telling him about it and how she dared not look her 'own mother' in the face and how Grace had passed her by without a word to help her and how that was what they had to do.

Grace was invited to her wedding but she did not come. She wrote such a firm and tender letter that Mary could feel neither offended nor guilty. Grace's teaching in Carlisle was going well: young lads would come up to her on the street and say, 'Hello, Miss. You learned me to read. Do you remember my name?' Dr Fraser relied on her increasingly and Agnes lightened her load by bringing in another woman to help clean and cook in the mornings.

When John was born, Mary wrote and Grace came to see him. 'And so there were the three of us,' John said to his mother. 'Do you remember when Grace came to see us?'

He remembered a few visits but they merged into one. He would be told, at the age of seven, or nine, or thirteen, until he left school, presumably once a year on or near his birthday, that 'Grace' would be coming. He would be given this information when he came back from school and his mother would make him wash his face and tidy up. Grace would be shown into the cold, underused sitting room and they would sit opposite each other at the table, which was covered with the dark green cloth. Between them there was a potted plant. His mother would retreat.

John knew that she was important in his mother's life. He knew that he was important in hers. But he did not know who she was or why she was there until he was sixteen when his mother told him that Grace had died 'of consumption'. She had gone to see her near the end and asked her to come and live with her so that she could be beside John and herself, but Grace had refused. Had they asked him to see her? They would all three have talked then, surely, said something at the last. Whatever it was it would have been a holding of hands. The three of them. A few honest words between them. After her funeral he saw his mother in grief for the first time.

What was Grace thinking when she sat opposite him in that parlour? This son of her daughter, this scarcely known son of her eternally distant daughter, who was always out of the room. Making tea? Fretting? Why out of the room? And what was the boy supposed to say? Did they talk to each other? What did they say?

Grace would surely have asked questions. And he would have done his best to answer but it was so strained. Even at the time. Looking back now, John could not square the strangeness of the three of them in the same house at the same time with the fact that they were mother, daughter and grandson, one blood and quite similar in the way they looked. Yet frozen in this still-life. What force society then must have had to keep them so apart, John thought later, three people who ought to have been together, familiar, friendly, in warmth, easy, giving and gaining. No. They were three independent figures temporarily assembled in that house.

And Grace knowing all about Mary and about John, and John knowing so little about Mary and nothing about Grace and yet put there, opposite her, like someone summoned from afar to an intimidating court and placed there for an audience. No, that was too formal. It was humbler and finer than that. And no again: it was not the surface of things that permeated his feelings. It was the unspoken that he remembered. He could return to it with warmth and liking for her. Later, as he dwelled on it, he searched in his memory for any evidence that she had recognised those unspoken feelings.

And then she would go. As far as he remembered, she never kissed him or shook him by the hand. But on the table she would leave an envelope containing a ten-shilling note.

Now and then. The three of them were together but apart; their life as a family was that.

How deep could shame and modesty and the compulsion to observe the ritual of secrecy go? In his mother it plumbed

245

the deepest reach of her nature. How strong could self-possession be? In his grandmother it could service a sort of torture. His own ignorance, John was to think, was such a loss. He would have liked to know her: he would have loved her and she him. How good that would have been. Now he had to make it up. Now he had to imagine her, just as, increasingly, he had to imagine his mother. Memory was not enough.

~

She woke in a slurry daze, her eyes all unseeing, her mind still in debt to sleep. She did not know who he was, this man, near her, smiling. But she was good-mannered.

'Hello,' she said tentatively.

'It's John.'

'Oh. Is it John? Oh, I'm glad.'

'It's me.'

'Hello me.'

'Yes,' he said. Maybe that was how it was for her now.

He took her cold, bony, large-veined, brown-speckled hand. 'I've been with Grace,' he said.

'Have you? Isn't that good? That's good.'

'And you. With you as well. All of us were together.'

'Isn't that good . . . ? Grace was . . . She was very nice, was Grace . . . She had a lovely look about her.'

'So did you. I always thought you were the best-looking . . .'

'Go away! No. No . . .'

'Do you want to go back to sleep?'

'Just for a little bit. Wake me up, mind.' Rather feebly, she shook her forefinger at him.

'I will.'

'Good lad.'

~

And that would be the best of it now. As her dementia fastened its grip, her anxieties and her fears grew and her only defence was sleep. Days of sleep.

There would come a time soon when all she could do was drowse and make soft, short sounds. He would put his head close to hers and take her cold hands in his. Her eyes would open but mostly find no focus, just look ahead. She was in no pain that he could see but what of that he could not see? 'It's so hard for me now,' she had said, just a few months before. At times, even then, she would sing, fragments murmured but the melody still recognisable.

Should he not help her find a way to go, to die? But then there would be a smile and a slight pressure on his hands from hers and all he wanted for her was that she lived as long as there was no suffering and as long as that which was in her kept this sweet, brave woman alive.

~

He stayed a while longer and then drove away, going first to Wigton where he wanted to look in on a friend.

He walked around the small town centre, which had once to him been a metropolis of alleys and cuts, streets, squares, yards; at night a jungle with muted sounds like a low wind muttering between the branches of the old town where low lights speckled feebly against the stars.

Now, at twilight, despite the mid-century gutting and transplanting of the place, John could conjure up what had been and see where Grace would have come as a girl and where Mary was adopted and protected by the intense closeness of it all. And where he as a boy felt that the world was all about him.

He walked along Water Street in the dusk and came to the Congregational church, no longer a church, just a property, still up for sale. Water Street, in his memory for ever a seething stream of skinny children, cattle being herded to the station, horses, women on the doorsteps, pigs squealing in their pens, upended bicycles being mended on the pavement. All gone now, a car park, an emptiness.

The door was ajar. He went down the stone steps and pushed it open to look in at the hall. In the far corner a woman was sweeping the floor. She looked up and nodded pleasantly but said nothing as he came in and sat down and looked around.

This was where they came. This was where they had danced. It is at this time, just after the war in the middle of the last century, that they still meet most happily.

～

He felt a deep but tranquil sorrow. All gone. The town now lost to the character of his own past there. Churches and chapels, little shops and narrow alleyways, common frugality and livestock inside the town itself, all gone, like so many of the people. Mary now only just holding on, himself next in line.

And yet as he sat there he felt a sweet sorrow, a sure recollection of a happiness taken from the grip of deprivation.